A Novel

THE
WEST
TEXAS
PILGRIMAGE

M. M. WOLTHOFF

RIVER GROVE
BOOKS

Published by River Grove Books
Austin, TX
www.rivergrovebooks.com

Distributed by River Grove Books

Design and composition by Greenleaf Book Group
Cover design by Greenleaf Book Group
Cover images: Chisos mountain ©jkauffeld/istockphoto.com; climbing a mountain ©bee_photobee/istockphoto.com; group of hikers ©Olga Danylenko/istockphoto.com; front rock ©IS_Imagesource/istockphoto.com

Lyrics from "Gringo Honeymoon," words and music by Robert Earl Keen. Copyright © 1994 BMG Bumblebee and Keen Edge Music. All rights administered by BMG Rights Management (US) LLC. All rights reserved. Reproduced by permission of *Hall Leonard Corporation.*

Cataloging-in-Publication data is available.

Print ISBN: 978-1-63299-071-6

eBook ISBN: 978-1-63299-072-3

First Edition

This book is dedicated to the Flying Burros and
Mr. Bob Conger;
if it weren't for him, there would be no burros.

We were standin' on a mountain top
Where the cactus flowers grow.
I was wishin' that the world would stop
When you said we'd better go.
—*Robert Earl Keen, "Gringo Honeymoon"*

————————

For those who suffer in silence, I hope you find
your peace of mind. Have faith in God that your
mountain in West Texas is out there somewhere.

CHAPTER 1

EL MUY GRANDE

It had been a slow afternoon in the blind. The only sign of life had been a two-and-a-half-year-old ten-point chasing a hot doe across the *sendero* and into the mesquite brush. Although his head-gear looked impressive, his lack of caution and underdeveloped body indicated his immaturity. Hunter looked down the dusty trail to the south and beyond the enormous gravity protein feeder that sat a hundred yards from his twelve-foot-high camouflage fiberglass enclosure. Cinco, Hunter's best friend, had corned the sendero all the way to the end when he had dropped Hunter off earlier in the afternoon, but nothing had come out to eat. The rut, that two-week timeframe when whitetail bucks lose all inhibitions in their quest for a breeding doe, was all but over, and the lack of activity confirmed it.

Hunter checked the weather on his iPhone. It was unseasonably hot for early January, even for South Texas, but the forecast called for a norther blowing in by evening. The winds were already picking up from the north, and he could feel the change in temperature, which had already dropped ten degrees in the hour that he had been sitting. When he climbed up into the blind, he had been comfortable in a short-sleeve shirt, but the chill in the air told him it was time to put on his fleece camouflage vest.

The phone vibrated, and a text message from Cinco popped up on the screen. "Anything?"

Hunter typed his reply: "nada mucho. saw a 2.5 yr old 10 pt chasing, you?"

The counter reply was nearly instantaneous: "2 pigs and an 8 point."

Cinco was on the other side of the ranch, sitting in his top-drive three-quarter-ton Ford with a space-age-looking blind in the back, where the bed used to be. It wasn't enough to be able to drive it from on top of the cab; Cinco had to have a blind that could be hydraulically raised twenty feet in the air. Hunter laughed when he thought about the cost of that toy and how deer must react when they see it coming.

He removed his camouflage baseball cap, ran his hands through his shaggy yet thinning dark-brown hair, and put the cap back in place. As he took a long pull from the Cuba libre he'd mixed before the hunt, he surveyed the landscape around him, making sure he wasn't missing anything moving. Normally a beer drinker during the day, he found that a rum and Coke was a good cocktail for the blind. He could sip it, get a good buzz, and not have to get out of the blind to piss like he would after several beers. A big deer would spook from the commotion of climbing out of the blind, and once he caught a whiff of human urine, he wouldn't be back anytime soon.

The slightly dimmed yellows and oranges on the horizon indicated the sun was setting over the White Ranch of Jim Hogg County. The sendero to his west opened up into a hundred-acre pasture that the White family had entered into the US Department of Agriculture Conservation Reserve Program—CRP—several years earlier. The program paid ranchers or farmers to designate land for native grasses and wildlife rather than farming or grazing it. This pasture of tall, brown grasses with a few mesquite trees mixed in had become a quail haven over the last few years, but the drought had nearly wiped out the quail population on the ranch. Hunter and Cinco had only seen two small coveys in the day and a half that they had been there.

Hunter S. Sharp was in his element. There was something about sitting in a deer blind by himself that was better than any therapy money could buy. He found a peace in the wild South Texas brush country that the city lights of San Antonio could never bring him. It was peace of mind that Hunter sought so desperately and that seemed to be increasingly hard to find. This was the first time in two months that he could think halfway clearly. When Ty Sanderson, one of his best friends since Hunter and his family had moved to San Antonio from The Valley prior to high school, lost his battle with cancer a month ago, Hunter started to feel his grip on his own well-being slowly slip away. Sleep had been the first thing to go, followed by increasing levels of anxiety that seemed to twist his insides up like a pretzel. Over time, a cloud of darkness had set in, along with a lack of interest in everything: work, relationships, family— anything that truly mattered.

When Robert "Cinco" White V, Hunter's other closest buddy from high school and fraternity brother at the University of Texas, suggested Hunter come down to the ranch before the weekend trip, he jumped at the opportunity. Cinco's family ranch was one of his favorite places, second maybe only to the flats of the Lower Laguna Madre, where he grew up stalking redfish. It would be a getaway before their group of friends said their final good-byes to Ty. In a world that seemed to be ever changing with careers, marriages, and all of the challenging aspects of facing life as an adult, Cinco had been a constant, always there for him. Hunter hoped Cinco's recent engagement wouldn't change their relationship. He'd hardly seen some of their close friends after they got married. He understood that priorities change over time, but all of a sudden, the hunting and fishing trips were less important than weddings, engagement parties, baby showers, and other seemingly endless social events. Cinco, who was already much more heavily connected in the San Antonio social scene than Hunter had ever been or cared to be, would inevitably be sucked in further by his equally well-connected fiancée.

Hunter tucked his hands into the pockets of his fleece vest, folded up his collar, and stared down the sendero while reflecting on how much life had changed. Hunter had graduated from Alamo Heights High School in San Antonio as an all-state linebacker, on his way to greatness at the University of Texas. Football, school, fraternity life, and increasing levels of personal struggle and internal strife had been too much to juggle, so he had decided to focus on partying and having fun. Unlike Ty, he had managed to do just enough to get by in school, which bought him four years of virtually no responsibility.

Beth, his high school girlfriend, had followed him to Austin, but they drifted apart because he couldn't commit to the relationship.

At the time, he'd thought staying together meant marriage for sure. Not only was he having too much fun to settle down, but he also didn't want to miss an opportunity for something better. Besides, it wouldn't have worked anyway because her family was weird; they didn't like football, didn't hunt or fish, and probably voted for Obama in '08. At least that's what Hunter told himself when he thought about her, which was often. Beth got married last July and apparently never looked back.

Then there was Ty. He had always been the toughest son of a bitch Hunter had ever met. Ty lived hard and fast. He had also graduated from Alamo Heights with Hunter and Cinco and pledged the same fraternity at UT, but that was where their paths diverged. Ty was never much into school. Hunter wasn't quite sure how Ty got through the first year, but he was absolutely positive that Ty hadn't attended a single class his sophomore year. Austin had a way of creating distractions for an eighteen-year-old. Ty was either planning the next party at the fraternity house, driving back and forth between Austin and his parents' ranch on the Devils River, or chasing women on 6th Street. Hunter couldn't count the times he'd gotten up to go to school to find Ty facedown on their living room floor or, even better, discovered that Ty had brought a new "roommate" home with him from the bars.

Ty certainly got the most of that year and a half, but it wasn't sustainable. When he failed out of school, he tried to stay around Austin for a semester, but his dad, a prominent San Antonio neurosurgeon, wasn't about to support his party lifestyle any longer. Ty enrolled at San Antonio Community College the next semester, but that wasn't for him either. There was a war going on in the Middle East, and Ty had never shied away from a fight. He had been talking about enlisting since he and Hunter had watched the Twin Towers collapse on September 11, 2001. In mid-2003, he enlisted in the army and went Special Forces. He survived two years in Afghanistan, but when he visited Austin on leave, Hunter could tell he'd changed. He still partied hard, maybe even harder, but there was a seriousness—or maybe a lack of ease—that had never been there before. Hunter remembered catching him in the thousand-yard stare that people say is typical of hardened combat veterans.

When Ty got out of the army and announced he was getting married to Jessica Williams from Dallas, a girl they all knew from college, it took everybody by surprise. The courtship could not have been very long, since Ty was constantly deployed. That was Ty: one hundred percent all-in at full speed, even when it came to falling in love.

A year later, in June, when Jessica was expecting Ty Junior, the most shocking news of all came by way of a late-night phone call. Hunter remembered that call vividly, because it was the first time he had ever heard fear in Ty's voice. Ty had been to a physician because he hadn't been feeling well. After several tests, he'd been diagnosed with acute myeloid leukemia. The prognosis was not good, and Ty was afraid he wouldn't be around to meet his son. Hunter, Cinco, all of their fraternity pledge class, many of Ty's army buddies, and most of the Alamo Heights community prayed for Ty to make it at least until his son was born. Ty Junior arrived in late October, and his daddy got to hold him. Although Ty had looked terrible, he was clearly overjoyed by the arrival of his son. Hunter couldn't help breaking down in tears when Ty asked him to be the boy's godfather.

Ty must have fought hard to get to October, because by

mid-November, he was going downhill fast. Cinco and Hunter said their final good-byes in Ty and Jessica's house on Elmwood in Alamo Heights on December fifth. Ty died surrounded by family in the early morning hours of the next day.

Hunter removed his dark-brown-framed Costa Del Mar sunglasses and wiped his welled-up eyes as he thought about that last night with his best friend. It had only been a month ago, and he could still see the look of defeat in Ty's eyes. He had fought to the bitter end, and it was the only battle he had ever lost. Hunter found the bottom of his Stripes forty-four-ounce mug and finished off the last of the rum. He felt he should get his shit together so he could be there for Ty Junior, who was going to need as many father figures as he could get. Thus far, Hunter hadn't been of much help.

The sun was setting, so Cinco would be coming to get him shortly. The low light at dusk required using optics to effectively see anything. Hunter gripped his Steiner binoculars tight and surveyed the sendero to the south. The temperature had dropped even further, and the deer would be on the move.

Deer hunting could be a lot like billfishing in that it could be hours of nothingness, leaving one to get lost in deep thought, which could break into pure pandemonium in a split second. If the hunter or angler wasn't prepared for that second when the big deer showed himself or the billfish knocked down a line, he may not get a second shot.

Something caught his eye on the edge of the sendero, just south of the feeder. He could barely make out heavy horns protruding out of the thick, light-green mesquite and black brush. A big-bodied buck stepped out onto the sandy path and peered back at the deer blind, as if to check whether Hunter was watching. One cautious look to the south and one more step out toward the feeder left the deer's massive body completely exposed. Hunter's heart rate rapidly increased as he tried to examine the buck's headgear through his binoculars. He carefully put down his Steiners and reached for his .270 Weatherby, where it rested against the corner of the blind. His grandfather had given him the rifle at his high school graduation. The Leupold three-by-nine magnification scope mounted on his rifle would certainly give him a better look at the monster now standing under the feeder.

Hunter leveled the wood stock of his rifle on the window ledge of the blind and adjusted the magnification of the scope to full nine power. The buck tilted his head back and buried his long nose in an arm of the gravity feeder, revealing his massive neck and chest. He looked worn out from the rut and had clearly lost weight, as his belly wasn't as low-hanging as Hunter would have expected on a mature buck. He was mature though; Hunter was sure of that. The massive horns, long snout, squinty eyes, and noticeably loose skin around his brisket indicated that he was at least six and a half. From his vantage point, Hunter could see six typical tall points of his left main beam. The G2 and G3 points, the second and third points on the antler up from the brow tines, were at least a foot long.

Hunter intentionally slowed his breathing, although he had no intention of pulling the trigger. He had not even chambered a shell in the rifle. The buck took a breather from eating the protein pellets and turned his massive head north toward the blind, allowing Hunter to see his right side.

"Oh my God," Hunter exclaimed under his breath. The deer was bigger than any he had seen on the hoof. The right antler had six tall typical points equal to the left side, with a drop tine hanging down off of the main beam that was at least six inches long, adding up to thirteen total points. Hunter estimated at least a twenty-five-inch spread between beams; he was as wide as he was tall. He did the math to get a Boone and Crockett score and realized that he was watching a 180-class deer.

Hunter focused the crosshairs in his scope on the buck's shoulder and imagined pulling the trigger. The biggest deer he had ever shot was an eight-point management buck on the White Ranch that scored in the high 140s.

This is your lucky day, brother. You can make it one more year, Hunter thought.

The buck must have sensed danger or got his fill of protein, because just as stealthily as the monster had appeared in the sendero from the west, he disappeared through the brush to the east. Deer like that never stick around long.

Something about watching the deer lifted Hunter's spirits and gave him some hope that things would get better. He took it as a sign from God to remain faithful. Although self-admittedly not a model Christian and despite relatively little actual knowledge of the Bible, Hunter believed in God. His faith may have been due to his surroundings growing up and the influence of friends with strong faith, or maybe it was because the alternative to God's existence was too scary a scenario. He said a quick prayer of thanks under his breath and reached again for his phone.

He texted Cinco again: "BIG deer at the feeder . . . you on your way? Need rum."

Cinco's reply came in seconds: "packing up and heading your way."

It was completely dark now, and the cloud cover hid the normally bright stars over the South Texas brush country. It was also considerably colder than it had been hours earlier, and Hunter's fleece vest wasn't doing the trick.

Cinco pulled up to the blind about fifteen minutes later. Hunter could see the headlights of the truck coming from across the CRP field to the west. He closed the windows, shouldered his rifle, and backed his way out of the blind and down the twelve-foot ladder, which was no small feat for his six-foot-one, 245-pound frame. When he opened the passenger's door to the truck, Hunter was relieved that Cinco was blasting the heater.

"What did you see, bud?" Cinco, a wiry five-foot-ten, leaned back in the driver's seat, reached out his right hand to grab Hunter's rifle, and positioned it between the passenger's seat and the center console, the barrel down toward the floorboard.

"Man, el muy grande." Hunter opened the rear door of the crew cab to find his bottle of Bacardi. "Biggest deer I've ever seen on the hoof," he said. "Thirteen pointer with a big drop tine, every bit one-eighty. Probably six and a half years old." He grabbed some ice from the cooler, halfway filled his Stripes mug with rum, popped open a Diet Coke to mix, and squeezed half of a lime into his Cuba.

"Damn, son!" Cinco said as Hunter climbed up into the truck. "Pull the trigger."

"It's not my fuckin' ranch, and that's a ten-thousand-dollar deer." Hunter knew better than to shoot a deer like that, particularly when Cinco was starting to sell hunts on the ranch.

"I've seen him on camera, and we saw him from the air earlier this year, but no one else has seen him on the ground." They always made an aerial game survey by helicopter prior to the deer season. "He's got at least one more year in him." Cinco took a sip from his

Coors Light longneck. "Let's go see what Gloria has cooking." He put the truck in gear.

CHAPTER 2

ALFREDO AND GLORIA

The White ranch house sat on the highest point—not really a hill—of the 3,200-acre property. It was once in the dead center of a 6,000-acre family ranch, but as often happens, generations of the White family disputed over the land, which led to a fence line just north of the house, forever splitting the ranch, which had been in the family for nearly a century. The north side of the former White Ranch had been divided into two smaller ranches and sold off. The initial split had been a bitter one, leading to lawsuits and bad blood. Cinco's father had represented the White family interests, whereas his father's aunt, Barbara White-Springer, and her two sons were on the other side of the courtroom. As soon as the Springer family started leasing their land to Houston-based hunters, Cinco's dad added to the fence, making it nine feet tall, to prevent the big, protein-fed deer on the ranch from crossing over and getting shot at young ages.

The single-story stucco house didn't look like much from the outside. The windows had black bars over them to prevent entry from unwanted visitors from the south who would be traveling through looking for food and water. There was a second house, also single-story and stucco, about one hundred yards east of the main house, where Alfredo and Gloria, the married couple who had worked the ranch all of Cinco's life, made their home.

When Cinco and Hunter pulled up, Alfredo was out in front of his house by the game-cleaning station, a cement pad with a rusted metal hand winch that controlled a rope pulley system used to lift animals off of the ground or out of a truck bed. Once hung up and cleaned, they could be swung into the enormous walk-in cooler on the other side of the pad.

"He's going to be disappointed in us," Hunter said as he saw the anxious look on Alfredo's face. No one cleaned game with efficiency and precision like Alfredo, a skill he had fine-tuned over the years of working for the White family.

"One cold beer and he'll be alright." Cinco always offered Alfredo a beer. It was only right since Alfredo had been buying him beer since he was fifteen. The boys stopped by the cleaning station and got out of the truck, drinks in hand.

"¿Nada?" Alfredo did look somewhat disappointed, even though that meant his work was done for the day.

"Nada, pero Hunter mira un muy grande." Cinco handed Alfredo one of his Coors Lights.

"¿Dónde?" Alfredo reached out his weathered hand to shake Hunter's, who was always impressed with the ranch hand's massive forearms and strong handshake.

"Siete," replied Cinco, indicating that Hunter had been sitting in the number-seven blind.

"¿Tú comes?" Cinco asked.

"No, pero la cena es listo." Alfredo motioned toward the house where Gloria had dinner ready for the two boys.

"Ustedes comen con nosotros," Cinco said, insisting that Alfredo and Gloria eat with him and his guest. Cinco's parents would never ask the couple to eat with them, but Hunter knew that Cinco felt as close to Alfredo and Gloria as to his own mother and father. They had worked for the family before he was even born, for more than thirty years, and although they could not travel north with the family to San Antonio because of the Border Patrol checkpoints, Cinco had spent as much time growing up on the ranch with them as he could. There were numerous times when Cinco's parents left him and his younger sister at the ranch with Alfredo and Gloria for a week at a time to go on vacation or business trips. To this day, Cinco talked to one of them over the phone on a weekly basis. He wasn't fluent in Spanish, at least proper-grammar Spanish, but then again, Alfredo and Gloria had their own brand of border dialect, their own Tex-Mex language that they communicated effectively with. Typically, that meant four or five words in Spanish followed by one or two in English.

Alfredo and the two hunters walked into the front door of the main house and picked up the familiar smell of venison cooking on the stove and homemade flour tortillas. Hunter was always impressed by the transition from the outside of the house, which didn't look like much, to the spacious and exquisitely decorated interior. The three-thousand-square-foot house wrapped around an inner courtyard that was enclosed except for a tall wrought iron gate and sidewalk that led to the garage and mudroom to the east. The courtyard and flooring throughout the house were stained concrete. Walls of glass and French doors opened out toward the courtyard, allowing natural light into the house. The twelve-foot ceilings offered plenty of wall space for the many trophy animal mounts displayed in every room of the house. Cinco's mom had been responsible for the Southwestern and Mexican-flavored décor.

Gloria was setting the dining room table when the three men walked in. She had already built a fire in the large stucco fireplace at the far end of the rectangular mesquite table.

"Siéntate," Gloria said as she pulled out a chair. She had made picadillo, a dish made of ground venison, peppers, onions, and fried potatoes that they would wrap in her homemade flour tortillas. Hunter was very familiar with the cooking that Cinco grew up on. While the boys were in college in Austin, Gloria would make enchiladas and chili rellenos for Cinco to bring home and put in the freezer. They made fantastic late-night food after parties or bars.

She delivered Hunter and Cinco's plates first, along with cups of steaming hot charro beans. "¿Qué quieres beber?"

Cinco pointed to his Coors Light. "Una más cerveza, por favor."

Gloria opened a small refrigerator hidden in the kitchen bar, pulled out another Coors Light longneck, and handed it to Cinco, who sat down at the table and removed his Brush Country Outfitters camouflage baseball cap, revealing almost bleached-blond curly hair. "¿Hunter, quieres algo a beber?"

Hunter held up his forty-four-ounce mug, which was still over half full of Cuba libre, and shook his head. "No, gracias."

"Siéntate y tú comes," Cinco told Gloria, indicating the chair next to him, which brought him a warm smile of appreciation from her. Hunter took notice that Cinco was always careful to not eat before both Alfredo and Gloria were sitting with their food; it must have been out of respect for the couple, who had devoted their lives to serving his family.

Hunter ate his picadillo taco and charro beans as he listened to Gloria and Cinco hold most of the dinner conversation. His Spanish wasn't as good as Cinco's, but he could understand more than he could speak. Gloria asked Cinco about his fiancée, Mia, whom he had proposed to at the ranch over Christmas. Mia had gone to high school with the boys at Alamo Heights, but she was three years younger. Cinco had started to date her after he served as her duke for Fiesta, a weeklong celebration in San Antonio that brings the city to a halt. She'd been a duchess in the Queen's Court of the Order of the Alamo.

Hunter never quite understood the concept of girls "debuting" in handmade dresses that were more expensive than luxury cars, but he certainly always appreciated the party that ensued. All it took was seven straight days of intense celebration, very little sleep, and Mia making her public debut for the young couple to know they were serious about one another. Blame it on Fiesta. Hunter had more than one buddy who ended up marrying their Fiesta dates.

Alfredo was a man of few words, but when the conversation turned to Nuevo Laredo and the violence happening in their home state of Tamaulipas, he joined the discussion. Nuevo Laredo was a highly contested entryway into the US drug market. Once the drug traffickers had access to I-35, they could distribute to any market in the country. Mexican president Felipe Calderón had declared war on the Mexican drug cartels back in 2006, and while the press celebrated individual Mexican Army victories, the violence throughout the country had escalated to unprecedented levels. It was not uncommon to hear about gun battles—either between Mexican forces and cartels or between rival cartels—and assassinations of political figures on a daily basis. To make matters worse, Los Zetas, an army developed by the Gulf Cartel in the late nineties, had taken control of Nuevo Laredo. The paramilitary group, made up of highly trained former Mexican military soldiers, was known for its brutal tactics and had the entire city in a state of fear. Alfredo commented that Los Zetas had grown too powerful and that their former employers, the Gulf Cartel, no longer had any ability to control them. He told of public beheadings and bodies hanging off of highway bridges with signage warning anyone who dared to take on the powerful drug cartel. Although he talked to family in Nuevo Laredo on a daily basis, he could not visit them, and the general consensus was that things were getting worse in Tamaulipas, not better.

As Hunter listened to Cinco and Alfredo talk about the impending war being waged fifty miles to the west of the ranch, he sipped his Cuba libre and wondered whether anything would ever be the same. It wasn't that long ago that he had been at the Cadillac Bar in Nuevo Laredo until three in the morning, without a care in the world. His sales territory with the physician supply company he worked for included Laredo, so he would make at least a monthly trip down south, stay at La Posada on the river, and walk over to the famous Cadillac Bar for late-night cocktails and to place a bet on whatever sporting event happened to be on the TV. His local customer base had been telling him for months that he should avoid crossing, but he had assumed it was an overreaction to isolated violence. The picture Alfredo painted told a very different story.

After dinner, Gloria washed the dishes, and Alfredo took the trash out to the dump. The couple operated like clockwork, always retiring to their casita at nine o'clock sharp. Hunter knew they would both be up at five in the morning, Gloria preparing breakfast and Alfredo sipping coffee in preparation for another day of mowing, checking feeders, feeding cows, maintenance, and anything else he could think of that needed to be done around the ranch. Cinco's parents were bringing a group of friends down to the ranch for the weekend, so the old couple would be even busier than usual over the next couple of days, making sure that everything was perfect for the Whites' visit.

Cinco walked over to the wet bar at one end of the kitchen, picked out a whiskey glass from a cabinet above the bar, filled it with ice from the machine, and poured a Scotch to the rim.

"You need another Cuba for the fire, bud?" he asked.

The courtyard had an outdoor fireplace that had originally been the fireplace in the ranch house, from the early 1900s. It was a long-standing tradition in the White family to end the night around the old fireplace with a whiskey drink and some good bullshit.

"Yes, sir. I'll take uno más." Hunter got up from his seat and handed Cinco his convenience-store mug. Cinco shuffled through the bottles in the bar to find the Bacardi and mixed a Cuba libre to the best of his ability.

"We need some tunes for the fire too," Hunter said, already plugging his iPhone into the stereo system in the adjoining living room and turning on the outside speakers.

Gloria had built the fire outside before dinner, so it only needed a little fuel to get it going. Hunter added a couple of mesquite logs to the burning embers and pulled up a metal lawn chair next to the fireplace. Cinco sat next to him with both drinks and propped his handmade ranch boots up on the hearth, stretching his legs. The boots were monogrammed with the Roman numeral V, representing his place in the White family lineage as Robert the fifth.

"Good to have you down here, bud."

Hunter sensed the tone of concern in Cinco's voice. They hadn't seen each other since Ty's funeral a month ago, and Hunter's withdrawal must have been a clear-cut sign to a friend who knew him well enough to recognize when he was not doing well.

"Thanks for having me down, brother." Hunter took a long pull from his Cuba and propped his boots up on the hearth at forty-five degrees to Cinco's. "I needed this."

"You doin' alright?" Cinco asked, although he clearly knew the answer.

"Yeah, man, but I haven't been sleeping very well. I keep thinking about Ty and his family. I mean, fuck, man. Why him?"

Cinco sipped his Scotch. "I don't think there is a why," he said after a minute. "Shit just happens. I mean, don't get me wrong—God has a plan—but do I think it was in the plan for Ty to die of cancer at twenty-six, leaving behind his baby boy? No, I can't believe that." He drank more Scotch, this time more than a sip. "I know one thing. Ty is going to be with us this weekend. He always talked about us doing this trip, and I'm pretty sure he's not going to miss this one. Have you ever been out there?"

Hunter kept his gaze on the fire. "His ranch is as far west as I've been. I always wanted to get out there with him, but never got the chance."

They both went quiet when "No More Buffalo" came on over the outdoor speakers. "Ol' McMurt knows how to write a song," Cinco said. Hunter was already thinking how appropriate the song was to kick off the weekend ahead. James McMurtry, son of legendary

Pulitzer Prize–winning author Larry McMurtry, of *Lonesome Dove* fame, had an amazing talent for capturing raw human emotion in song lyrics. Hunter could identify with his often deep, dark music. McMurtry was one of his favorite songwriters. "No More Buffalo" seemed, to Hunter, to be about an old soul traveling through the West only to find that the Old West was no more.

In the morning, they would be heading for Ty's family ranch on the Devils River, northwest of Del Rio, where the Texas Hill Country meets the wild frontier of West Texas. There, they would meet up with two close friends and Ty's dad on Friday to push west to Marathon and Big Bend National Park, a trip that Ty and his dad had taken on an annual basis since childhood. Hunter distinctly remembered Ty saying that the closest he had ever been to heaven was with his dad at the top of a mountainous peak in Big Bend.

"You're gonna love it out there," Cinco said. He had only been out to the park once before, but he had made several trips out to that part of West Texas to look at ranches for his real estate business. "You feel like you're away from everything. It's wild, kind of like the last frontier." The excitement was evident in his voice. "I mean, it's a place people go to get off the grid, to disappear."

Hunter liked that thought. "Man, disappearing sounds pretty fuckin' good to me."

The conversation quickly turned to University of Texas football and the near comeback that a freshman quarterback had engineered against the University of Alabama in the National Championship game a few days earlier. They agreed that Garret Gilbert wasn't prepared to play in the first half when Colt McCoy went down with an injury but that he almost pulled it off in the second half. Neither of them had flown out to Pasadena for the game, but many of their fraternity brothers had made the trip.

The fire had burned down to embers after a few more McMurtry songs and a brief debate over which girls Cinco thought Hunter should be chasing. Cinco took one last gulp of Scotch and melted ice and stood up from his chair.

"Big day tomorrow," Cinco remarked. "Headin' west for a little cultural exchange in Ciudad Acuña." They had decided earlier in the week that they would go out to the Sandersons' ranch a day earlier than the rest of the group and have a night out in Acuña, the Mexican sister city to Del Rio. They'd both been to Acuña several times with Ty when they were in college, and they thought that they'd better not break their tradition of dinner at Ma Crosby's and drinks at the Corona Club.

"I'm right behind you, brother. I've got a little Cuba to finish up here." Hunter leaned his head back as Cinco headed off to bed.

"Buenas noches," Cinco said as he disappeared into the dimly lit house.

The next thing he knew, Hunter woke up to barely smoking embers and what was left of his Cuba libre dripping onto his lap. The temperature had dropped again. He could see his breath, and although he had on a ranch-style work coat, he was no longer warm. He looked down at his watch and realized he had been out for two hours, roughly the average amount of sleep he was getting these days. Getting back to sleep would be a challenge. He rose slowly from his chair and oriented himself toward the French doors. Inside, he turned off the music and clumsily found his bedroom. He stripped down to his boxers and got as far underneath the thin layers of sheets and blankets as he could to warm up.

The room seemed to slightly spin. He closed his eyes, and he could see Ty in his last few hours of life. His thoughts moved on to Beth, his missed opportunities in football, and how the world seemed to be rapidly changing around him. He had no idea what he wanted to do with his life, but he was sure that his current job selling physician supplies was not it. The money was decent, and through a combination of having an established network of San Antonio physicians and decent interpersonal skills, he had been reasonably successful, but the thing was that he had no desire to climb the corporate ladder, and selling supplies to physicians interested him only as much as the commission checks that came with the sale.

It was becoming harder and harder for Hunter to distinguish rational from irrational thought. Although he was learning to cope with his bouts of depression and extreme anxiety—recently diagnosed as symptoms of obsessive-compulsive disorder—that had plagued him for several years, the last six weeks had been extremely hard. Contrary to the stereotypical symptoms and behaviors portrayed in Hollywood, the OCD manifested itself in repetitive negative and intrusive thoughts, completely irrational in nature, with compounding anxiety as he failed to not think them. The futile effort to stop thinking about something was like pissing in the wind. The literature pointed to exposure to the thoughts and fears as the only effective treatment, but that was a lot easier said than done when the "what if" contained in those thoughts scared the hell out of you. Old anxieties had spiked to new levels, and a cloud of depression had settled in. It was like someone had sucked the joy out of everything he loved. He had been through it time and time again, so he knew it was temporary, but at its worst, it could feel completely overwhelming and demoralizing.

After an hour of ruminating, the O in OCD fully manifesting itself, the only thing Hunter wanted was sleep. He knew it would be hard to come by this weekend, so he had really hoped to get a decent night's sleep at the White Ranch before the trip. Sleep could make all the difference in the world for his ability to cope with the depression and anxiety. He got up from his bed, found his way to the bathroom, and fumbled through his dopp kit to find his sleeping medication.

There were some advantages to working with physicians all day. He had mentioned to one of his primary care docs that he wasn't sleeping and immediately received a script. It seemed to counteract the activating effects of the SSRI he had also been recently prescribed. Although the warnings on the side of the pill bottle read not to consume alcohol in conjunction with the medication, he had taken them after much heavier drinking than tonight's and had never had any issues. He took one of the pills, pounded a bottle of water that had been left for him on the bathroom sink countertop, and made his way back to bed. Hopefully, a good night's sleep would bring some peace of mind.

CHAPTER 3

ROAD TRIP

The next morning, Hunter woke to the sun flooding his bedroom window. He looked at his watch and was pleasantly surprised to see that it was after eight. That meant he had slept for an additional five hours, which was by far the most sleep he had gotten in a long time. His head was still a little fuzzy and ached slightly from the rum, but all in all, he felt pretty good. Nothing a Bloody Mary couldn't fix. He slowly rose out of bed and made his way to the shower. The concrete floors were cold on his bare feet, which made him move a little quicker. The hot water of the shower was a welcome relief.

Cinco had been up for several hours. He'd had a cup of coffee with Alfredo and Gloria, and then he and Alfredo took a vuelta around the ranch. Cinco was staring out the courtyard window when Hunter walked into the room, fully dressed but obviously fresh out of the shower. His slicked-back, soaking-wet hair appeared much darker than it actually was. "Buenos días, brother," Cinco said. "There's eggs and tortillas in the warming oven. Coffee's fresh."

He proceeded to tell Hunter about his early morning stroll around the ranch with Alfredo. Apparently, the two of them had been up for hours, sipping coffee, corning the senderos, and glassing deer with binoculars from the hunting truck. Alfredo had most of the mature bucks on the ranch named and had spotted several of them. This morning's lineup included "Cabrón," the big twelve-point that was clearly a dominant buck in the herd because he scared off all the other bucks when he was out and about, and "Señor Rocky," the ten-point that was missing half of his right G2, the second horn off of the main beam from the head, which had probably got broken off in a fight.

"It's a beautiful morning, bud." Cinco sipped his coffee. "Chilly, but not a cloud in the sky."

Hunter went for the coffeepot first. "You hanging out in here by yourself?"

Cinco didn't look at Hunter but replied, "I was thinking about the last time Ty was here. I've been avoiding thinking about him, with everything going on over the holidays, but sitting here this morning, I remembered that bird hunt in September. It was too damn hot for Jess—eight months prego—and Ty looked like shit from his treatments, but they came down anyway. He said he just wanted to see 'em fly. Said he really appreciated a good South Texas white wing flight and wasn't going to miss it this year. Mia shot his limit for him, and he was standing right here later when he told me to quit fucking around and to put a ring on her finger. I told him I was working on it." Cinco kept his gaze on the window. "How'd you sleep?"

Hunter slicked back his wet hair once again and sipped his coffee.

"Other than the two-hour nap I took outside with my Cuba in my lap, I slept pretty good, man. Ready for the weekend."

Cinco laughed. "You better be ready, bud. Things are fixin' to get real western."

Hunter made his plate, poured another cup of coffee, and sat down across from Cinco. "So what's the game plan?"

Cinco shifted his eyes from the courtyard to Hunter to answer. "Well, I figured if we get on the road in an hour or so, we can be at their ranch by three or four. We'll check in there, and then we'll be having 'ritas at Crosby's by dinnertime."

"Sounds wueno," he said, dropping the b, "but I need a Bloody before we do anything." The taco and coffee wasn't enough to relieve Hunter's headache. He finished up both and took his plate to the kitchen sink. "You want one, man?" Hunter was shuffling through the bottles in the bar to find the vodka and already had two Styrofoam cups on the counter before Cinco answered.

He stretched and nodded. "Yeah, if you're gonna have one, might as well make two. I wasn't planning on boozing until later, but if you're gonna twist my arm."

Hunter scooped both cups into the ice machine, overpoured the vodka, and went to the refrigerator for the Clamato, Worcestershire sauce, and lime. A little Tabasco and a dash of pepper completed the mix.

Cinco grabbed his drink from the kitchen counter. "Well shit, might as well take them as roadies. Let's go ahead and get moving."

Hunter was way ahead of Cinco and had already packed. He had three bags with him on top of the carrying case for his rifle: a King Ranch leather overnight bag, his camouflage hunting gear bag, and a King Ranch vinyl boot bag where he kept his Lucchese full-quill ostrich boots. He was wearing his bull-hide ranch boots, which had a seventeen-inch shaft that went up almost to his knees, a one-and-a-half-inch cowboy heel, and his initials stitched into the front. He had them custom made by a bootmaker in Raymondville after he wore out his first pair of Chippewa snake boots. He liked them better than the Chippewas, because he could wear them all the time and still have some protection against snakes while on the ranch. The Chippewas had been designed to be worn with the pant legs tucked into the rugged snake-guard shaft of the boot; they weren't the most fashionable thing to wear out on the town.

Hunter put his gun case on the back floorboard of the crew cab and his bags on the leather backseat of Cinco's three-quarter-ton long-bed Chevrolet. Everyone in his family drove white trucks, claiming that the South Texas pinstripes—scratches created by the sharp mesquite brush—were less visible on white than they were on any other color.

"Leave some room for a cooler, bud." Cinco was right behind him with a big leather bag in one hand and a soft cooler of equal size in the other. "I filled her up with ice, but we need to pick up some beer when we fuel up." He also had a Yeti cooler locked into the bed of the truck. It still held twenty pounds of ice from the day before. Within five minutes, they were loaded up and climbing into the Chevy to start their adventure west.

The whine of the diesel engine was clearly audible through the open windows as Cinco slowly navigated the caliche road out to the main gate. Hunter plugged his iPhone into the stereo system and played Willie Nelson's "Bloody Mary Morning" at a low volume so as not to hurt his head any worse. The air was crisp, and it felt great inside the truck with the windows down. Both Hunter and Cinco had put on their Costa Del Mar sunglasses to reduce the glare of the bright morning sun. Hunter sipped his Bloody Mary and hoped his headache would go away with every drop. At the end of the road, Cinco clicked the opener clipped to the sun visor to open the big steel gate, rolled up the windows, and pulled the truck out onto Highway 16, heading north toward Hebronville.

Once they hit the Hebronville city limits, Cinco pulled into a Valero gas station with a Stripes convenience store. He left the truck running as he slid out of the cab, swiped his credit card, and started the pump. He leaned back against the side of his truck, crossed his legs, sipped his Bloody Mary, and appeared to be taking in the Thursday morning scenery.

Hunter was amazed at how busy the store was. Like every other Stripes in South Texas, this one housed a Laredo Taco Company, a made-to-order taco grill. It seemed like everyone in town must have stopped by the Stripes for their morning breakfast taco. It was no wonder that obesity and diabetes plagued South Texas more than anywhere in the country. "Welcome to the Hebronville Mall," Cinco said from the other side of the truck.

Cinco had finished pumping and pulled the truck up to the front of the store by the time Hunter got through the line with a twenty-pound bag of ice and two cases of Lone Star Light cans. He filled up the soft cooler, put everything else in the Yeti, and climbed back into the truck.

Cinco dumped what was left of his Bloody Mary, kept the Styrofoam cup as a spittoon, and broke out his can of Copenhagen snuff. "You want one, bud?" He offered the open can to Hunter first.

"No, sir. I'm trying to quit." Hunter hadn't had a dip in several weeks, and he was trying to stay strong.

"Suit yourself, but it's a long way to the Devils River."

"Don't worry about me, man." Hunter lifted his cup. "I've already got my buzz back from last night, and I'm not planning on losing it."

The truth was that Hunter was afraid of coming down for too long and ruining the weekend. Hangovers were not exactly conducive to working through a bout of depression, so his theory was to drink through it and deal with it after the trip. He knew it would be incredibly difficult when the time came. His biggest fear was ruining the trip for his buddies, for himself, and especially for Ty. He buckled in his seatbelt and finished what was left of his Bloody Mary as Cinco pulled out onto Highway 16 heading north toward Freer.

They were in Freer in half an hour. Cinco wanted to stop at the Muy Grande Village, at the intersection of Highway 16 and Highway 44, to find out who the leaders were in the annual Muy Grande deer contest. The contest, which got its start in 1965, was well known throughout South Texas, and hundreds of hunters entered every year. Cinco planned on entering this year even though he hadn't yet harvested a buck, and he was interested in sizing up the competition.

They walked into the gas station turned store, restaurant, and contest headquarters to view the enormous leader board that covered two entire walls, floor to ceiling. There were eleven divisions, including men's, women's, youth, Mexico, low-fence, and the "Macho Grande," and within each division, there were several categories, such as widest spread, overall score typical, and overall score nontypical. Just about every category had an entry this late in the season and, true to form, there were some monsters.

"Look at this dude." Hunter pointed at a picture of the nontypical deer leader, which grossed over two hundred inches. The massive buck had more than twenty antler points. Cinco was clearly
more interested in the ranches that were producing the leaders than
the actual deer themselves. Many of the ranches listed were direct
competitors to his new hunting operation that he and his dad were
getting started on the White Ranch.

"Los Orcones and the Parr family are on the board," Cinco
pointed out. Hunter recognized the name as the famed Parr family
ranch in Duval County. The Parrs were known nationally for their
political machine in the early to mid-twentieth century. George
Parr, also known as the second Duke of Duval, was infamous for
his role in the Box 13 scandal, the rigging of a 1948 US Senate
primary election that resulted in Lyndon B. Johnson, on his way to
the presidency, beating Coke R. Stevenson by an unbelievably slim
margin. The truly unbelievable part of it was that there were 202
late votes from a single precinct in Duval County's neighboring Jim
Wells County, all in alphabetical order, and all deceased at the time
of the primary election. Twenty-seven years later, among multiple
scandals and a ten-year prison sentence for tax evasion, the legendary Duke of Duval killed himself on the Los Orcones. Hunter had
heard many stories over the years about the Duke of Duval from
Cinco's dad.

One *vámonos* and the two were out the door and in the truck
again, this time headed west on Highway 44 toward Encinal.
Along the way, they encountered the daily flood of oil and gas
tankers and every support service that the Eagle Ford Shale boom
had brought to South Texas. It had been almost two years since
Petrohawk Energy had discovered the oil and gas productivity

of a geological formation that would lead to one of the biggest economic events in Texas history. Once-sleepy South Texas towns were now bustling with activity as land men looked to buy up oil and gas leases, production companies came in to drill and hydraulically fracture—otherwise known as fracking—and roughnecks flocked to the rigs for work. Hotels were full, restaurants were full, gas stations were full, and, perhaps most noticeably, the highways were full. Everyone from everywhere was flooding to the area to get a piece of the action.

The traffic on 44 forced Cinco to slow down to below the speed limit of seventy-five and follow the endless line of trucks to Encinal and I-35. Both Cinco and Hunter got a kick out of the bumper sticker on the beat-up Ford dually truck in front of them that read, "I love," represented by a big red heart, "Eagle Ford."

Hunter reached back to the soft cooler and pulled out his first Lone Star Light. "If we're going to be stuck in traffic, might as well drink some cold beer."

"You go for it, bud." Cinco spat into his Styrofoam spittoon and smiled. "You know you're driving home tonight from Acuña." Going back to college, Hunter had always been the driver for their group of friends, regardless of alcohol intake. Amazingly, he had managed to get through unscathed—not that he had never been pulled over. At the time, he wore that responsibility like a badge of honor and rather ignorantly saw it as a test of manhood. He was one of very few in their group of friends without some form of an alcohol-related offense, whether it be DUI or open-container citation. To this day, partly out of superstition, his buddies would still rely on him to get them home in a pinch.

"Man, I've got to come up with some service that caters to these guys down here. This place is a goldmine right now." Hunter was always looking for new business ideas that could potentially relieve him from selling supplies to physicians.

Cinco kept his eyes on the crowded highway. "Good luck finding something that hasn't already been thought of. I hear someone is putting in a titty bar in Encinal. When Encinal has a titty bar, everything else has been covered."

Hunter tried to come up with services that may not have already been provided and came up blank. "Where in the hell do they find strippers in Encinal, Texas?"

Cinco looked over to answer this one. "Where there's oil and natural gas, there's money; where there's money, there's strippers. I'm sure they'll come from Laredo or SA. We'll have to see for ourselves when they open up."

Once they passed under I-35, Encinal came and went in the blink of an eye. Another twelve miles and Cinco had the truck heading north on Highway 83. At no point did the traffic let up as they drove into the heart of the Eagle Ford Shale activity. Cinco pointed out the simple stone pillars and wrought iron gate of George Strait's ranch about fifteen miles south of Catarina. On that note, Hunter dialed up "Blame It on Mexico" on his iPhone and grabbed another Lone Star Light from the soft cooler. By noon, they'd made it to Carrizo Springs, where Cinco took a left onto Highway 277.

About forty-five minutes later, Cinco pulled the truck into a Mexican food restaurant on the north side of Eagle Pass. They didn't know where to eat lunch, but this particular hole-in-the-wall was busy with locals—Hispanic, not gringo—and they sold cold beer, which sealed the deal. No one in the restaurant was speaking English.

They were pointed to the only available table for two, in the corner. Cinco ordered two cheese enchiladas, an iced tea, and a Modelo Especial. Hunter also went with a Modelo Especial, since they didn't sell Lone Star, and the beef enchilada and beef taco combination plate with charro beans instead of refried. The soupy concoction of pintos, peppers, onions, bacon, and anything else the cook could throw in were named after charros, or Mexican horsemen. Hunter had always preferred charro beans to refried, which went back to his family's maid, Diana, when they lived in Harlingen prior to moving to San Antonio. She made charro beans with nearly every meal, and they were always fantastic.

Their food came out in less than ten minutes, but Hunter had already drained his first Modelo. "Ma'am, I'm going to need another cerveza to wash this food down," he said to the waitress. He was pretty sure she only understood "another cerveza." The food was as good and greasy as they expected it to be. They were anxious to get on the road and get to the ranch, so there wasn't much small talk between bites at the lunch table, and they both took down everything on their plates in a manner of minutes. As Cinco finished his last bite of enchilada, he waved the waitress over and requested the check: "La cuenta, por favor."

The waitress gave him a warm smile, clearly pleased that he spoke to her in Spanish. "Sí, señor."

As they were climbing back into the truck, now a shade of off-white from all of the dust, dirt, and monstrous bugs they had collided with along the way, Cinco read aloud the road marker ahead on Highway 277: "Del Rio, fifty-five miles. Almost there, bud! Hand me a cold beer while you're back there."

Hunter reached back into the soft cooler and was disappointed to find that there were only a few Lone Star Lights left in the backseat of the truck. "Let me refill the cooler before we get movin'." He jumped out of the cab, put his right foot on top of the rear tire, and lifted himself over the side rail of the bed to reach the Yeti cooler. After shoveling several beers into the soft cooler, he was back in his shotgun seat, holding a cold beer for each of them.

Highway 277 north between Eagle Pass and Del Rio brought a huge contrast in landscape. After hundreds of miles of South Texas brush country, they could tell they were extremely close to the Rio Grande River as they passed through the Quemado Valley and the irrigated farmlands that surround it. The town of Quemado had seen better days, primarily indicated by the population sign that read 243. On the north side of the valley, and as Highway 277 veered further away from the river, the terrain turned back to the familiar arid brush land. They both commented on the constant air traffic from the Air Force base located just east of Del Rio. Neither of them was very familiar with military plane types, but they did know that the Del Rio base trained pilots. Ty's family had hosted many of them at the ranch over the years.

It had been a couple of years since either of them had been through the town, and they were surprised to see the development on the north side. "Man, Del Rio has gone big time. I mean, holy moly, a Chili's, Home Depot, and a Rudy's Barbeque," exclaimed Hunter.

"You could sell to physicians out here, bud. Settle down with a little chiquita, live on Amistad." Cinco's sarcasm was evident in his tone of voice.

"I'd do it in a heartbeat," Hunter said, "but it's too far from the coast. I'm not a bass fisherman." He'd always felt San Antonio was too far from the salt water at two hours by land vehicle; Del Rio would be an extra haul that he wouldn't be willing or able to make as frequently. "I mean, I know it would be a long way to the fuckin' country club," he said, using the same degree of sarcasm. Cinco, through a sponsorship by his parents, had recently joined the San Antonio Country Club. The thought of spending the kind of money it took even for the initial deposit to become a member— roughly the cost of a brand-new boat or truck—was ridiculous in Hunter's eyes.

Cinco laughed out loud. "Don't be bitter you're not in the club."

Just outside of town, Highway 277 and Highway 90 diverged, with 277 breaking off to the north. A gas station stood at the fork. Sacks of deer corn were stacked up to the roof on either side of its front door, and several chickens were running around out front.

"Now that's the Del Rio I know and love," Cinco said. "The turnoff to the ranch is twenty miles from the fork."

"Ten-four, Mr. Country Club. Need another beer?" Hunter had already grabbed two more Lone Star Lights from the cooler. They crossed Lake Amistad at about 2:45, and the green water looked beautiful beneath the sun and crystal-blue sky. The man-made lake was known for its clarity and often hosted scuba divers as well as bass fisherman. In fifteen minutes, they turned west onto an unmarked dirt road.

The name of the Sandersons' ranch, Rancho El Flujo Del Rio, translated as "the flow of the river ranch." The entrance gate was unmistakable. It stood about five miles off the highway on the left of the winding road. The sign stood at least nine feet tall and had the ranch brand—"F–R," pronounced F bar R—in one-foot-tall letters right in the middle. Cinco pressed the button on the electronic security system to call the headquarters. After several rings, a gruff voice answered. "Cole, it's Cinco White and Hunter Sharp. Sorry; we forgot the code."

Cole Johnson, the ranch foreman, was out driving around in one of the many ranch vehicles, but he had the ability to let them in remotely from his cell phone. "I'll meet you boys at the head-quarters. Come on in." The tone in his voice became much more friendly when he realized it was Cinco and Hunter, two of Ty's buddies whom he had hung out with on the ranch on multiple occasions. Nearly instantaneously, the massive gate slowly swung open, and Cinco crept the truck through.

CHAPTER 4

F-R

Hunter was always amazed at the vastness of the F bar R. Ty had never told them exactly how big it was, and the truth was that he probably hadn't known himself. Ty's great-grandfather on his mother's side bought the ranch back in the twenties with a piece of the small fortune that he had made in the oil business. The first thing anyone visiting the ranch noticed was the three-thousand-foot asphalt airstrip north of the main ranch road. Ty's family had always loved to fly, and it became the preferred method of transportation to the ranch from their Houston home. A little farther west, the stables, where the family kept their collection of horses and mules, stood south of the road. Ty's mother and her sister, the two living inheritors of the ranch, had grown up on horseback and still frequently rode. Ty's younger sister, Stacy, also developed a love for horses and grew up riding.

The headquarters, better described as a compound overlooking the Devils River, was what really made the F bar R special. The five-thousand-square-foot main house, the three-thousand-square-foot hunting lodge, and the pool house were three separate Spanish hacienda–style facilities lined up on a sheer cliff above the river. The views were spectacular from every angle, and the west-facing sides of the buildings were mostly glass.

As Hunter and Cinco pulled up to the huge circular driveway, they couldn't help talking about the good times they'd had there with Ty. The first time Hunter had been to the ranch and the first time that the three of them had been together at the F bar R was their sophomore year in high school, and they had made regular trips there ever since.

"It's weird being here without Ty," commented Hunter.

"I know, brother. We've had a lot of good times out here. Let's focus on that." Cinco chugged the rest of his beer and opened his door to step out of the truck.

Cole pulled up five minutes later in his brand-new white full-ton Dodge pickup. He was a big ol' boy, almost as tall as Hunter and twice as thick. He wasn't that much older than Cinco and Hunter, but his were a weathered thirty-five years. The lines on his face and in the corners of his eyes reflected a constant beating from the sun, and he kept his thinning hair short and neat to help hide the gray that had taken over the black. Hardly anyone saw it since he was always wearing his beat-up grey Resistol. He was missing a thumb on his right hand, which he had lost in a roping accident as a teenager. He was a second-generation ranch hand; his dad had also worked for Ty's mother's family for years prior to retirement.

Cinco dropped his bag and went to shake Cole's hand. "It's good to see you, Cole," he said.

Cole removed his aviator-style sunglasses. "Glad you boys made it." He extended his huge thumbless hand to Cinco. "Make yourselves at home in the lodge. I've got beers iced down on the porch. Mrs. Sanderson and Stacy are coming in by dinnertime. Are you planning on eating here?"

Hunter hadn't known Stacy was going to be there. "No, sir!" he quickly said, unsuccessfully trying to mask his discomfort. "We're heading to Crosby's for dinner. You want to come with us?"

Cole appeared to be tempted but definitely hesitant. "I haven't been over in a while," he said, "but I've got to get the pit going for the women, and I have a few other things to do before they get here. I know how nights in Old Mexico go with you boys." Cole used to drive Ty and his buddies around Acuña and had been along for many a wild night.

Cinco must have sensed the hesitation in Cole's response. "Are we good to go in Acuña? Nuevo Laredo is a mess."

Cole adjusted his silverbelly hat by pulling slightly on the brim. "Yeah, y'all should be alright. It's a little rougher than it used to be. I'd probably stay away from La Loma." He was referring to "The Hill," otherwise known as Boy's Town—the red-light district of Acuña.

Hunter smirked at that counsel. "We don't even know where that is."

Cole didn't look amused, which took Hunter by surprise. He gave the two a look of concern and asked, "Y'all need help with anything?" They declined the offer and carried their bags and Hunter's deer rifle into the lodge.

The inside of the hunting lodge was nicer than most people's homes. The front door entered into a great room with mounts of every kind of game animal imaginable, a full-size kitchen, a wet bar, a pool table, and a huge flat-screen TV on the wall. A Saltillo tile floor led to glass French doors. The doors opened onto the back porch, which overlooked the river. There were two bedrooms downstairs and three bedrooms upstairs that surrounded the great room in a loft configuration. Hunter led the way up the stairs to one of the bedrooms, which contained two bunk beds and familiar pieces of western art depicting cowboys and Indians in a time long past. Both of them had stayed in this room before, so they decided not to break tradition.

"What in the hell was that look on your face when Cole mentioned Stacy coming in tonight?" Cinco said. "Did you two hook up or something?"

Hunter looked sheepishly back at him.

"You did! It's about time. That girl has had a thing for you since you moved to SA. Did you fuck her?"

Again, Hunter did not reply.

"Oh my God. You fucked Ty's little sister, and she's coming here tonight. This is awesome." Cinco was clearly enjoying this conversation more than Hunter.

"We got all boozed up after the service," Hunter explained, "and we were the last two at the bar. Things just happened."

Cinco laughed again. "She likes to party, bud, just like her big bro. What's the big deal?"

"I haven't talked to her since. I told her I would call her, but I haven't."

"Nice work," Cinco said. "Well, this will be awkward."

Both of them changed to long-sleeve, button-down shirts, which they tucked into their Wrangler blue jeans, and donned their gray felt hats to get ready for their night out. Hunter's hat was a standard Resistol 4X western, with a four-inch brim blocked in the front, that he'd had since high school, and it had the battle scars to prove it. Cinco's smaller three-and-a-half-inch-brim hat was custom made from the renowned Texas Hatters in Lockhart. It was made of one hundred percent beaver fur, the best hat-making pelt available. He had it made to mirror the hats that his father and grandfather wore while working cattle on their South Texas ranch.

Cole was already sitting at the giant circular mesquite table with a Coors Light bottle in his hand when they stepped out onto the porch. The table had hosted many poker games over the years and even more bullshit sessions. "Don't y'all look pretty," he said. Cole had always given Ty and his buddies hell about being "pretty city boys" from San Antonio.

"Big night in Acuña tonight," Cinco said with a straight face. "We've got to dress like we know what we're doing."

Both of the "city boys" pulled up a chair to the table. "What's been going on up here, Cole?" Hunter envied Cole's lifestyle at the F bar R and hoped to get a peek into the ranch hand's experiences.

"Not a damn thing. Been pretty quiet since the rut ended and I saw you at Ty's services. We had a group of oil company executives up for New Year's. Some dumbass Houstonite gut-shot a two-and-a-half-year-old ten-point. Of course, he expected me to track it and clean it, and all he wanted was the head for a skull mount." It was clear Cole wasn't always fond of the company that Ty's family kept.

"Seen any big deer this year?" Cinco sipped his Coors Light.

"The drought has hurt, but Danny, Ty's cousin, shot a stud during the rut," Cole said. "He was a six-and-a-half-year-old ten-point that scored in the one-seventies. There's another big boy, at least twelve points, out there that we've collected sheds on the last couple of years and seen on camera at night, but nobody has seen him during the day. Ty was hell-bent on hunting that deer this year. We've also seen more big sheep this year than in years past." He was referring to the herd of Aoudad sheep they had on the ranch.

Having already drained his Coors Light, Hunter grabbed three more from the trough that had been turned into an ice bucket by the outdoor kitchen on the porch. "Well, Cinco's got some big news," he said with a hint of sarcasm.

"I got engaged over Christmas," Cinco said. "We've been dating since Fiesta last year."

Cole once again took off his aviator-style sunglasses and looked at Cinco with an inquisitive glare. "Well, I don't know if congratulations or condolences are in order, but either way, here's to ya!" He extended his bottle toward Cinco's for a quick "Cheers!" and took a long swig.

"She's a good girl," Cinco said. "You'll like her. She can definitely rough it at the ranch."

Hunter found Cinco's definition of "roughing it" and his half-hearted effort to defend his decision to get engaged equally amusing.

"Remember that time our freshman year when Cinco, Ty, and I brought three dates out here?" Hunter said. "We coupled up in deer blinds and had a bet on which girl could shoot the biggest doe. Cinco and I came back with deer, but Ty and his date came back with an empty bottle of Jim Beam. They were so hammered they couldn't figure out how to put each other's clothes back on right!"

The reality was that during a fraternity-sorority mixer in the middle of the week the three guys had convinced three girls from Abilene, whom they hardly knew, to pack overnight bags and drive out to Ty's ranch with them. An overnight trip turned into a three-day hiatus from school. It had been only a few years back, but it seemed so long ago.

Cole laughed. "That was the chick who was dancing on the table at Corona Club that night, right?"

Cinco chimed in: "Yes, sir. She was the smoking-hot one too. The other two weren't quite as fun as she was."

Hunter found comfort in the storytelling. It was the first time he had been able to laugh and mention Ty in the same breath since his friend's last days. He sensed that the other two realized the same therapeutic value of their conversation.

Hunter knew that Cole had always viewed Ty as a younger brother and had treated him as such. Cole hadn't shown any emotion throughout the services or around the family, but it was painfully obvious that he hurt as bad as anyone over Ty's death. He commented that he had seen Ty at the ranch in September before the baby was born but didn't realize it was going to be the last time he would see him. Cole expressed sincere regret over the fact that he didn't have the opportunity to drive into San Antonio to say good-bye.

"Cole, you going with us this weekend?" Hunter didn't know whether he had been invited to go or not, but he hoped so.

"Yes, sir. I never went on this trip with Ty and Dr. Sanderson, but I'm sure as hell not going to miss this one."

Cinco put his fist out to meet Cole's for a pound. "Glad to have you on the trip, brother."

Two more rounds of beers and the sun was starting to set over the Devils River. Hunter loved watching the sun go down and had always thought that the sunset over the Lower Laguna Madre from South Padre Island was his favorite. This one, on this particular day in Southwest Texas, rivaled them all. Hunter once again thanked God for this perfect moment, just as he had the night before when that huge deer came out on the sendero and let him get a good look at it. As a lover of the outdoors, he couldn't understand how anyone could doubt God's role in its creation. When nothing seemed to be going right in life, with depression and self-doubt sinking in, the little things that Hunter could find joy in gave him hope to find peace of mind. He also had faith that Ty was there with them; he wouldn't have missed this moment at the F bar R on the Devils River for anything.

Just before the sun was completely below the horizon, Cole got up from his seat. "Boys, the women will be here any minute now, and I need to get to work. Y'all better get on the road." He shook their hands. "Watch out for DPS out there. See y'all in the morning, and don't get too fucked up." He headed for the main house to prepare dinner for Mrs. Sanderson and Stacy.

Cinco looked at Hunter with a sarcastic smile on his face. "We better get out of here before things get weird for you, bud."

Hunter didn't reply but was in total agreement.

"I've got to take a piss; then, let's vámonos." Cinco was already halfway through the back door.

Hunter took one last look at the picturesque scenery and followed him into the hunting lodge. He might as well take a leak now too and get it over with. You can do just about anything in Mexico, but pissing in public isn't one of those things. He knew this firsthand; one of his pledge brothers had been hauled off to jail for urinating on a light pole outside of the Corona Club on a pledge trip to Acuña.

Five minutes later, they were checking Cinco's truck for shells.

"Check under the seats. I haven't cleaned this thing out in a while." Cinco pulled out his floor mats, looked underneath the driver's seat, and opened up his console. Mexican customs randomly searched vehicles, mainly looking for one of two things: guns and ammunition flowing into their country. Hunter had heard horror stories about hunters going over to Mexico for dinner, forgetting that they had shotgun shells or other unused ammo in their vehicle, and getting their vehicles confiscated, never to be seen again. Once they were satisfied the truck was clean, Cinco was back in the driver's seat, and they were headed east on the unpaved road toward the highway.

Hunter had restocked the soft cooler in the backseat for the half-hour ride to the border. With the tunes now playing at a higher decibel, they were fired up about another night in Old Mexico.

"Man, I'm glad we did this." Hunter's gaze was fixed out his open window as he took in the cool evening breeze. "This was a great idea." The afternoon of drinking and reminiscing coupled with the prospect of a big night in Acuña had him feeling high.

Cinco extended his beer over to Hunter's to give him a cheer, "Just like old times, brother. Ty wouldn't have wanted us to do it any other way."

CHAPTER 5

VIVA ACUÑA

"Really?" Cinco said and eased the truck forward. "How is there rush hour traffic in Del Rio?"

"You in a hurry?" Hunter said. "We've got plenty of cold beer and good tunes. Mexico isn't shutting down anytime soon; we'll get there when we get there." He dialed up ZZ Top's "Mexican Blackbird" on his iPhone, which was connected to the stereo system again. "Here's a tune to get you fired up about Acuña."

Five minutes later, they were over the train tracks and in Del Rio's old downtown. A sign for the Val Verde Winery reminded Hunter of a couples' trip he and Beth had made to the F bar R in college to hang out with Ty and his date for the weekend. He and Beth spent the entire afternoon at Texas's oldest winery and most of the night in Acuña at the Corona Club. They had blacked out after dinner and had no idea how they got back to the ranch, but it was another occasion when Cole had saved the day and driven into town to pick them up at the border. That was during their sophomore year, the weekend Beth had given him an ultimatum: Either commit to the relationship, or she would move on. Hunter had often wondered how things would have turned out if he had said yes. There was no point in wondering about that now. Those days were long gone.

Cinco followed the Highway 277 signs to Ciudad Acuña and pulled over into the last gas station before the bridge to get cash from an ATM inside the convenience store. He quickly jumped out of the truck but turned back. "Can't ever have enough cash in Mexico, bud. You never know what you're going to need it for."

Hunter knew he was right, and, although he was hesitant to pull a lot of cash out of a checking account that was pretty much already drained, he reluctantly followed Cinco into the store. Once they had both had their turn at the cash machine, they were back on the road, heading toward the river.

Hunter was surprised to see so little traffic going into Acuña and very few cars in the lots where those who chose to walk over the bridge could park. Cinco pulled right up to the tollbooth and paid the pleasant elderly Mexican woman in uniform the small toll for crossing the bridge.

"Tengan cuidado," she said. Her advice to be careful made Hunter a little uneasy.

As they crossed the river, Cinco finished his beer and said, "Get rid of that beer, bud. I don't want customs giving us a hard time tonight."

Hunter pounded his Lone Star Light and tossed the empty into the soft cooler. "Mexicans don't give a fuck about alcohol," he said. "Cross your fingers for a green light."

The entrance to Acuña had two speed bumps and then a small traffic light mounted to a road sign to the left of the driver. Green meant that you were free to go; red meant your vehicle would be inspected. Hunter was always anxious as he approached those lights, often praying for green, even though he had nothing to fear from Mexican customs agents other than a little harassment. Cinco slowed to a crawl for the speed bumps. The light turned red.

"Damn it!" Cinco said. "Well, here we go." He took a left to get in the inspection line, which, like the Texas side, wasn't very busy. Two customs agents approached the truck. The older one, who had a thick, black mustache, approached the driver's side while the other one and his dog started a tour of the outside of the vehicle. Cinco rolled down his window to greet the older agent, who was clearly the superior of the other one. "Buenas noches, señor."

The agent's stern facial expression did not change. "Hablas español? Salgan del vehículo."

Cinco turned to Hunter and instructed him to get out of the truck and open both doors on his side. Both of them quickly got out and stepped away from the agents as they scoured the truck. The agent with the dog pointed at Cinco's leather seats in the back, and the dog responded by jumping into the truck and sniffing the cooler and other loose items on the backseat. The agent unzipped the cooler and held up the empty beer cans for his boss to see and then promptly put them back in and zipped it up again. Hunter couldn't help laughing, because the agent had proven his earlier point; they really weren't concerned about alcohol.

Cinco shot him a serious, disapproving look as if to say, Quit fucking around.

The senior agent finished his inspection of the inside and outside of the truck and then turned to Cinco and pointed at his black diamond-plate steel toolbox in the bed. The toolbox and the extra diesel fuel tank took up almost half the bed, and the box itself was easily big enough to carry multiple firearms. As Cinco unlocked the box and lifted the lid to let the customs agents do their inspection, Hunter caught a look of panic on his friend's face. Sitting on a tray in plain sight was a single twelve-gauge shell that must have fallen out of a bird bag at some point.

Mustache man picked up the shell and looked at both of the young gringos. "This is no good," he said in broken English. "We find any more, you go to jail."

Hunter instantly sobered up at the thought of going to a Mexican jail on the night before the West Texas trip. They'd forgotten to check the toolbox before leaving the ranch, and he was sure that there had to be more than one shell inside. He said a little prayer in his head, pleading with God that they wouldn't find any more ammunition.

The customs agents shuffled through tools, jumper cables, and various pieces of clothing for what seemed like an eternity to Hunter. When they finally gave up the search, the senior agent waved them back to the truck and muttered, "Pase," as he made his way to another vehicle that had been pulled over.

They hopped into the truck and pulled out of the inspection station as quickly as they could.

"That was a close one, bud," Cinco said. "No way there is only one shell back there. Someone is looking out for us tonight."

Hunter could tell from Cinco's tone that his nerves were frayed. He let out a nervous laugh. "All I know is I'm getting fucked up tonight."

Cinco took a right on Calle Bravo and then an almost immediate left on Miguel Hidalgo, the main street for restaurants, bars, and stores. Calle Hidalgo, with famous bars like Ma Crosby's, Corona Club, Up and Downs, and Pancho's, was where locals and visitors from across the Rio Grande came to party. The street was almost entirely as Hunter had remembered it—although he couldn't totally remember most times he'd been there. The bright neon lights and loud music of all different genres coming out of the bars and dance clubs seemed the same as they always were, except for the presence of the roadblock.

In the middle of the street sat an armored personnel carrier, facing away from the border, with a fifty-caliber machine gun mounted on top, which was manned by a young soldier, no older than eighteen. There was something unnerving to Hunter about a kid with a big machine gun pointed in their direction, just yards away from his vantage point in the passenger seat of Cinco's truck. He also noticed the general lack of activity on the street. He remembered a vibrant Calle Hidalgo that was busy whether it was three in the afternoon or three in the morning. "Man, it looks like things are a little tense over here."

"They're not looking for us. We're fine." Cinco kept his eyes on the military vehicle, now in his rearview mirror. "Let's go fill up with diesel before dinner."

Cinco told Hunter that he knew there was a Pemex nearby. Diesel was considerably cheaper in Mexico than across the border, and he could fill up the fifty-gallon tank in the bed of his truck to make the trip out west a little less expensive. He took a left and pulled into the gas station. They didn't have pay-at-the-pump, so Cinco walked into the storefront to pay while Hunter stayed with the truck.

Hunter couldn't help thinking that it was a little eerie that there was so little activity. He had read about people not leaving their homes after sundown in the other border towns, more in the middle of the emerging turf war between the various cartels, but he couldn't imagine that violence in Acuña had reached that point. Maybe it was just a slow Thursday night. Cinco came strolling out of the store toward the fuel pumps. "Come on, cowboy," Hunter called out his window, "we ain't got all night. Ma Crosby's 'ritas are calling my name."

Cinco pumped seventy-five gallons of diesel into his tanks and then jumped back into the cab. He pulled down on the short brim of his hat and said, "Get fired up, bud. Next stop is Crosby's."

They headed south to a one-way street, Calle Francisco I. Madero, which ran parallel to Hidalgo back toward the border. Cinco took a quick left, went five blocks past closed tiendas and dentista offices, and then took another left back toward the main street. They were looking directly at the enormous Ma Crosby's neon sign strung over the road. Cinco turned left on Calle Matamoros, which had the restaurant on the corner, and found a roadside parking spot on the curb.

They hurriedly jumped out of the truck and made a beeline for the front door of the famous bar and restaurant that had been serving both sides of the border for nearly a century. They couldn't avoid a little nostalgia on seeing the old pictures and mementos hanging on the wall. Two older Mexican men were sitting at the bar, talking to the bartender over their beers. The maître d' came out of nowhere from the restaurant side and, in good English, asked if they were planning on having dinner. They responded with an excited yes. He extended his right hand to Cinco for a shake and made a polite bowing gesture.

"Welcome to Crosby's," he said. "Follow me to your table."

The dining room was a great room with tables of all different sizes covered with white linen tablecloths. Aside from a Mexican family having dinner, no one else was in the room, which made it feel even bigger. Hunter ordered the first round of margaritas and queso flameado as they took off their hats and sat down. Hunter scooted his chair back from the table so he could cross his right leg over his left and took a good look around the room. "Man, I can't believe it's so dead. We've basically got the place to ourselves."

Cinco nodded. "It's a little creepy, for sure. At least the service will be damn good." They went silent for a couple of minutes, taking in the atmosphere and reliving old times, when tables were hard to come by in this iconic establishment.

Their waiter interrupted the silence, delivering the two margaritas on the rocks, two glasses of water, and the menus. Confident that it had come from a bottle, Hunter downed his glass of water, which he'd desperately needed after a full day of drinking.

Cinco lifted his margarita glass and said, "Salud, brother! Here's to one more night in Old Mexico."

Hunter raised his glass. "¡Salud!" He took down nearly half of his margarita.

It was only a couple of minutes before the waiter was back. "Are you listo?" he asked.

Cinco answered for them both: "Sí, estamos listo." Hunter ordered another round of margaritas and asked for the cabrito. Slow-cooked goat was one of his favorite dishes. Cinco went simple, with the combination plate—enchiladas, crispy tacos, and a chalupa.

The second round of margaritas came out within minutes, and the music switched mid-song to George Strait's ballad "Blame It on Mexico," which specifically mentions Ma Crosby's. Someone behind the bar must have recognized them for what they were: two gringos looking to relive good times. Hunter grinned and finished the first margarita.

"Man, these sons of bitches know exactly what they're doing to us." Cinco laughed and pretty much polished off his margarita as well. "It's what we're doing to ourselves."

A member of the waitstaff came by every five minutes on the dot. They seemed overjoyed to see the two Texans in their restaurant. Cinco asked one of them if this was the type of business they'd had recently, and he explained that yes, it had been this slow for some time. Few of their regular customers from Del Rio were coming over for dinner anymore. The staff's biggest fear was that they might have to close the restaurant side of the business after lunch.

"We'll do our part tonight," Hunter dryly assured the waiter.

The food came right after the third round of margaritas was served. It was just in time for Hunter, who needed something in his stomach aside from tequila and lime juice. Sometime after the second margarita, he hit that sweet spot between a good buzz and passing out and vomiting on himself. The trick was staying in that sweet spot, and a little cabrito to soak up some of that booze would help prevent the wheels from coming off of the train prematurely.

They became more talkative as the margaritas kept coming, and the volume level of their conversation rose as well. The Mexican family had left sometime between the first and second margaritas, so they had the restaurant to themselves. The staff didn't seem to mind their banter. By the time they had finished their meal and their fourth round of margaritas, they insisted that the waiter, Louis, take a shot of tequila with them at the bar.

Louis looked at them inquisitively and asked, "¿No quieren postre?"

Cinco looked at Hunter who shook his head. He was full from dinner and thought the dessert would put him to sleep. Louis politely declined the offer for a shot, but Hunter wasn't going to take no for an answer. Once they paid their bill and tipped him generously, Louis reluctantly gave in and followed the two cowboys into the bar. They ordered three shots of Cazadores, because they liked the big deer pictured on the label and because it was made in Arandas, in the state of Jalisco, the birthplace of tequila. Cinco handed the bartender his iPhone and asked him to take a picture of the three of them as they took their shots.

Hunter was the first to raise his shot glass. "¡Viva Acuña! ¡Salud!" he said.

They touched glasses and shot the one-hundred-percent blue agave tequila. Louis, unlike Hunter and Cinco, didn't need a lime, and as soon as he could say "gracias," he disappeared back into the restaurant.

As Cinco counted out dollar bills to pay for the shots, Hunter perused the stickers on the mirror behind the bartender. Most of them were squadron stickers from the Air Force base in Del Rio. He remembered buying drinks for pilots on several past visits to Crosby's, when the bar was full of people from every walk of life.

Hunter and Cinco walked out of Ma Crosby's as a third rendition of "Blame It on Mexico" started to play. Hunter sang along out loud as they headed catty-corner across the street to the Corona Club. The faint scent of sewage, an unfortunate characteristic of Acuña, wafted about them in the cool winter breeze. It was a bit sobering for both of them as they made their way to the next bar.

The Corona Club was always the second stop—and often the last—on a night out in Acuña. It had gained its claim to fame with the filming of the movie *Desperado*, with Antonio Banderas and Salma Hayek, in 1995. Many photos and mementos from the movie still hung on its walls. Deer shoulder mounts and horns filled the rest of the wall space. The bar was a square set in the middle of the Saltillo-tiled floor. The room had big brick support arches running right through the middle of it. On the side of the room opposite the entrance, through another set of arches, was the dimly lit dance floor. On good nights, there was always drunken, shady behavior on that dance floor.

Being at the club made Hunter miss Ty, whom he'd never been there without. It also brought back memories of Beth, who, on several occasions, had matched him at the bar drink for drink. Some of their best times had been nights in Acuña and, in particular, at the Corona Club. One night stood out to him: when Robert Earl Keen, Hunter's favorite songwriter and musical idol, played in the courtyard out behind the bar. Their group of friends drove down from Austin to meet Ty, who was home just before a deployment, and they'd all gone to see the show.

Hunter had talked Beth into making the trip with the guys even though she ended up being the only girl, which she took in stride. It had been during an extremely rocky point in their relationship—near the end, when they were fighting more than having fun—but that weekend had been different. Beth had known how much going to a Robert Earl Keen show at the Corona Club meant to Hunter, so there were no serious discussions about life plans or commitments. She went with the flow, and that was the flow of lots of booze. Her casual attitude and seemingly careless front that weekend almost made Hunter want to make that commitment she had been asking for.

Remembering floating with Beth that afternoon along the section of the Devils River just south of the ranch put the image of her in a bikini in his head. She had amazing curves; everything was perfectly proportioned to her medium-height build. She had put up with a full day of drinking, sexual innuendos, and general harassment from all of his friends. Not only did she put up with it, she gave it right back to them.

After an amazing dinner at the ranch, they talked Cole into driving them to the show, because none of them could put a sentence together, including Beth. The deal had been that Cole would drive them there, but they would need to get a cab to a hotel in Del Rio after the show, because he couldn't stay.

The show was amazing, as all Robert Earl Keen shows were; Hunter had never been to one he didn't like. He and Beth danced to nearly every song, which helped sweat out the booze a little to keep them upright. Once the show was over, they continued to dance on that dimly lit dance floor to everything from AC/DC's "You Shook Me All Night Long," which was a staple at the Corona Club, to rap songs by Outkast and Snoop Dogg.

They shut down Corona Club and found themselves dancing at an upstairs open-air bar to some conjunto tunes. When the rest of the group found them sometime between four and five in the morning, they were using the bar to support themselves while making out. The group collectively decided to forego the cab ride to Texas and walk the five blocks to the Best Western Villa Real in Acuña.

After Hunter and Beth paid for a room, they made a mad dash

for it, Ty and several other buddies in hot pursuit. Hunter slammed the door in Ty's face as he was trying to get inside. Beth was naked before Hunter could even turn around. It was the last time they had sex, and it was probably the best time, in his book. She was wild that night, and they went at it for three hours.

They may have slept an hour or so before showering and walking out to face the painful morning sun. The guys were in the lobby, drinking coffee and waiting for them to wake up. They had decided to go back out and drink until the sun came up instead of paying for another hotel room. Hunter later found out they'd all taken a taxi to Boy's Town for a couple of hours of tipping strippers and God knows what else.

The trip back to Austin that afternoon had been brutal. When he dropped Beth off at her apartment, he told her he would call her, but he didn't. Looking back, he didn't know why he hadn't called her or made an effort. Maybe it was the combination of the booze and the depression, maybe just immaturity, but he didn't even try. It was a hell of a way to treat an old friend who had been closer to him than anyone else. Evidently, it was the final straw for Beth, who had really been making all the effort to maintain the relationship. She stopped trying, and they drifted apart.

"You still with me, bud?" Cinco brought Hunter back to reality with a Modelo Especial from the one bartender working.

"Yes, sir. Just remembering old times. We've had some good times in this place, for sure." Hunter didn't want to get into the specifics of his thoughts, because he would have to mention Beth. They sat down on two stools at the bar, facing the empty dance floor, sipped their Modelos, and soaked in the atmosphere. From behind, the two of them in their felt hats must have looked like something straight out of an old western scene—two cowboys sitting in a Mexican cantina. There were a couple of old men on the other side of the bar, but like Crosby's, the place was virtually empty.

Cinco struck up a conversation with Rudy, the extremely overweight bartender, who claimed to remember them from years past. Rudy assured both of them that things picked up over the weekend and that there were always a lot of good-looking women on a Saturday night, even the kind of woman who would do almost anything with you for a reasonable fee. He reached under the bar and pulled out a stack of pictures to prove his point. Hunter and Cinco laughed as they shuffled through the Polaroid pictures—clearly not taken recently—of beautiful women in string bikinis on a stage outside and then some of drunken college-age girls on the dance floor inside.

"Nice pictures, Rudy," Hunter said. "Do y'all still do the bikini contest?" He had no hope of getting a straight or truthful answer.

"No, not this year. Next year." Rudy, who coincidentally reminded Hunter of Cheech Marin, the actor who played the bartender at this very bar in a scene in *Desperado*, seemed overly confident in the contest's fate.

Cinco had texted Mia the picture of the tequila shot at Ma Crosby's before they had walked into the Corona Club, and his phone beeped with her reply: "BE CAREFUL. Love You."

He texted back: "Love you too. Talk to you in the morning."

Cinco was now clear for the evening, with no further obligation to check in, which, he told Hunter, was a weight off of his mind. He ordered another round of Modelos.

After five or six rounds of Modelos and more conversation with Rudy than they would have preferred, Cinco turned to Hunter with a very serious expression. "Brother, I think it's about that time."

Hunter nearly fell as he stepped down from his bar stool. "Yes, sir. I think it's that time. Boy's Town?" He'd been waiting for Cinco to make the call. They hadn't really discussed making a trip to what locals referred to as the "Hill," the cluster of brothels southeast of town, particularly after Cole's warning earlier in the day. But it occurred to both of them that it was a good idea somewhere between the margaritas and the tequila shot at Crosby's.

Every Mexican border town had its own Boy's Town, and both Hunter and Cinco had spent time in nearly every one of them along the South Texas border. Hunter was pretty sure Cinco had lost his V-card in Eagle Pass, but he would never admit to it.

Hunter and Cinco said adios to Rudy and walked back across the street to the truck. Cinco tossed his keys to Hunter. "You know the way, right, bud?"

Hunter laughed as he climbed up into the cab. "Man, I've got a nose for it. Roll your windows down."

The reality was Hunter needed fresh cool air to clear his head and sober up enough to navigate the truck through the streets. He had never actually driven to Boy's Town himself, but he'd ridden shotgun on several occasions with Ty. He knew the rule of thumb was to head south until you hit a dead end, and then to find the highway that continued south out of town.

Hunter plugged in his iPhone and pressed play. Waylon Jennings's "Ain't No God in Mexico" came on. He turned the volume up loud enough for everyone on the street to hear, put the truck in gear, and headed south.

Hunter had only made it five blocks when he noticed a car with lights mounted on top marked Policia sitting on the right-hand side of the one-way street. He instinctively slowed down, but as he passed the cruiser, the lights flashed on, and it pulled out into the street behind him.

"Fuck, man, I don't think I was speeding." He turned down the volume of the stereo and pulled into the open parking lot of a hierbaría.

Cinco looked over his shoulder and said, "They're fucking with us, bud. Ask 'em how much they need."

The younger of the two police officers came to the driver's window and shone a flashlight into Hunter's eyes.

"¿Cómo estás?" Hunter said, trying to break the ice.

"You were speeding," the officer said. He had a very stern look on his face.

"Sorry, sir. I didn't think I was speeding." Hunter tried to avoid speaking directly to the officer, which would surely make his alcohol-soaked breath more noticeable.

"Come back to the car with me." The officer opened the door of the truck and gestured for Hunter to get out.

This took Hunter by surprise and sent a million thoughts racing through his mind, everything from *We're going to Mexican jail* to *Are they really police officers and should I get out of the truck or make a break for it?* He looked at Cinco for guidance and got a nervous nod in return.

He decided to follow the instructions and carefully got out of the truck, mechanically walked to the police car, and turned to try to keep the police officer from getting in between him and the truck. The second officer didn't say a word but was carefully watching the passenger side of the truck, in case Cinco were to try something.

After what seemed to be hours, the younger officer broke the silence. "I smell tequila. You have to go downtown."

Hunter could feel the blood drain from his face. "How much do I owe you?" he asked passively, his heart racing.

"¿Mande?" The officer clearly heard him, but didn't seem to understand.

"¿Cuánto necesitas?" This got an eyebrow raise from the officer.

"¿Cuánto tienes?" The officer wanted to know how much he and Cinco had.

Hunter guessed at the right number: "¿Ciento?"

"Ciento cincuenta."

Hunter breathed a deep sigh of relief and said, "Bueno." He pulled out his wallet and handed the officer $150 US, most of what he had, trying to conceal what was left. He knew he was getting off easy, but he didn't want to pay any more than he had to.

The police officer had one more question for Hunter: "¿Dónde van?"

Hunter fought back a smile and replied, "Boy's Town."

"La Loma?" The officer grinned widely as he opened his car door and gestured toward Hunter. He insisted, in Spanish, that Hunter and Cinco follow them. Hunter wasn't exactly sure what was happening, but he was just drunk enough not to question it. Back in the truck, Cinco peppered him with questions: "How much did it take, bud? What did he say? What in the hell is he doing now?"

The police car pulled out onto the street, lights still flashing, and slowly passed the truck. "He said to follow them." Hunter started the truck and pulled out to follow.

"Seriously? Follow him where?"

Hunter slyly grinned. "Boy's Town, man. I just paid one fifty for a police escort."

"You've got to be fuckin' kidding me. He's taking us there?"

"Yes, sir."

The two-car entourage continued south on Calle Matamoros until it came to a T, where the police car turned right and then made a quick left onto Boulevard Vincente Guerrero. Hunter recognized the signage to Eagle Pass, Saltillo, and Monterrey and knew they were on the main highway headed south, which was exactly the way to Boy's Town. This put to rest any doubt in his mind that the shady police officers were taking them somewhere else.

The next memorable milestone was the Plaza de Toros, on the outskirts of town. He and Ty had always talked about catching a bullfight there, but they'd never gotten the chance. The familiar stucco arch that spanned the highway, almost as if it were a gate to the city of Acuña, told him that they were close. The police car, lights still flashing, turned perpendicular in the middle of the highway, half in the northbound lane and half in the southbound lane to create a road block. The younger officer got out of the car and waved at Hunter to turn left in front of him. Hunter followed the instruction, waved to his newfound friend, and pulled onto the winding dirt road that led up the hill. A little sign on the right side of the road indicated that they had arrived.

Cinco was still in a state of disbelief. "I can't believe we got a police escort to Boy's Town. I mean, did that really happen?"

Hunter could hardly manage a reply through his hysterical laughter. "Man, he just liked me, I guess."

Acuña Boy's Town consisted of two big clubs with a small restaurant in between them at the bottom of the hill and several poorly maintained smaller bars at the top of the hill. Hunter and Cinco were only interested in going to one of the clubs, Hunter's Ranch. Just referred to as Hunter's by the locals, it wasn't only the name that appealed to Hunter. The bar was by far the nicest, in terms of facilities and girls, of all the options. The buildings, the women, and the clientele got progressively rougher the further uphill you ventured. Hunter pulled up in front of the bar, virtually front row, put the truck in park, and asked, "How much cash do you have on you?"

Cinco pulled out his wallet and thumbed through his cash. "One fifty."

"I'm down to fifty, so I might need you to spot me." Hunter opened his door and started out of the truck.

Hunter's Ranch was exactly as they had remembered it: deer mounted on the walls, a few stages for the girls, and lots of high tables around the stages. The bar was the first stop. Cinco ordered two Modelos, and they found a table in front of the center stage. There were several girls sitting in the back of the room, but no one was on stage yet. There were only two other occupied tables: Several older men who looked like they had been there a while occupied one, and two well-dressed younger men—definitely no older than Hunter and Cinco—sat at the other. The younger men seemed to be throwing around a lot of money to the girls in their laps.

A song that neither Hunter nor Cinco recognized started playing loudly, and a short, dark-complected dancer with remarkably large breasts for such a tiny body and wavy, jet-black hair down to her shoulders came out from behind a wall on the stage and strutted toward the pole by their table. She wore a red bra, which came off in seconds, and a bright red thong. Although her facial features didn't look Indian, her darker complexion indicated she was Mestizo, a genetic combination of Spanish and indigenous people, which was the ethnicity of a majority of the Mexicans in this region. She couldn't have been more than twenty years old, and although she wasn't toned, her legs and stomach revealed little fat. Her red, six-inch heels made her seem taller than she was, but she couldn't have been more than five feet tall. As she wrapped one leg around the pole, her dark eyes locked in on Cinco. She seemed to focus on him as she provided a show for everyone in the bar.

"Man, she likes you," Hunter said. "Give her some singles."

"I'm on it." Cinco was already reaching for his wallet and getting out of his chair to stand next to the stage.

Hunter got up to use the men's room. After a few steps, he looked back to see the dancer with her legs wrapped around Cinco's torso and him tucking one dollar bills into her thong.

The men's bathroom was nice by Acuña standards. Hunter had just finished pissing into the trough-style urinal when someone approached him from behind. He turned and saw an older Mexican gentleman with a thick, dark mustache and a white guayabera standing between him and the door. Hunter made a What do you want? expression.

"¿Quieres cocaína, cowboy?" the mustache asked. "Make you go all night long."

Hunter laughed. "No necesito. Gracias." He had never done cocaine, but the combination of an antidepressant and booze was enough to significantly delay an orgasm; he didn't need additional help.

"Good price," the dealer said. "What about your friend?"

"You can ask him." Hunter brushed by the man.

Back at the table, there were three new Modelos—one for him, one for Cinco, and one for the girl with the red thong, who was now wearing Cinco's hat and sitting at the table, topless. "Maria, meet my buddy, Hunter," Cinco said.

"Nice to meet you, Hunter," Maria said in perfect English, which surprised Hunter.

"She went to Del Rio High School, bud," Cinco said.

Maria smiled endearingly at Cinco and turned back to Hunter. "I'm from Acuña, but my grandmother raised me in Del Rio. I'm glad y'all came in tonight. Those old guys were creeping us out." She leaned closer to Hunter. "What kind of girl are you looking for?"

He blushed at the question and wasn't sure exactly how to answer other than looking around to try to point someone out.

"Look at him," Cinco said. "He's a beast. He needs a tall, skinny girl with great legs and a nice ass. He's always been an ass man."

Hunter had been in the middle of sucking down about half of his Modelo and almost sprayed it through his nose from laughing so hard.

"You need to talk to Veronica," Maria said. She got up from her chair, slowly ran her hand up Cinco's leg, and then walked back behind the stage.

Maria returned holding hands with one of the most beautiful women Hunter had ever seen. She had to be close to six feet tall, had long and wavy dirty-blond hair, a much lighter complexion than Maria's yet still olive-colored, and dark-brown eyes. She was wearing an off-white bustier and thong. Her legs looked like they went on forever.

Hunter looked at Cinco. "Holy shit," he said. "This is trouble."

The two girls approached the table. "Hunter, this is Veronica,"

Maria said. "She doesn't speak English as good as I do, but she understands it."

Veronica sat down at the table, crossed her long legs, and smiled at Hunter. "Mucho gusto."

Hunter wasn't sure whether he was really drunk or whether she was as hot as he thought she was. It was hard to believe that a girl who looked like she did worked at the club. He asked, "¿De dónde eres?"

"Monterrey," she quickly replied. "¿Y tú?"

Hunter told her he was from San Antonio and pointed to his beer. "¿Quieres una bebida?"

Veronica nodded her head and asked for a vodka and Red Bull. By the time he had returned to the table with the round of drinks, Maria was in Cinco's lap, dancing to another song. Cinco had his hands on her breasts from behind and didn't even notice Hunter had brought another round. Hunter handed the vodka drink to the voluptuous Veronica, who gave him her sexy smile in return.

"What are you doing here?" he said. "You could be a model." He wasn't sweet-talking; he was being completely sincere.

She put her hand on his shoulder and leaned in and said, "Thank you. You're sweet."

It was clear that either she didn't want to or she didn't know how to answer the question, and Hunter wasn't going to press the issue. He was quite sure that a beautiful Mexican prostitute like her had a jaded past that she probably didn't want to share.

Veronica took a long drink from her cocktail and then got up from her seat at the start of a new song. Without saying a word, she moved in front of Hunter's chair and started to dance for him. Her long legs and perfect figure moved in sync with the rhythm, and Hunter couldn't help reaching out and pulling her in closer to him, which she didn't resist. Sitting in his lap, she moved to the music while he moved his hands up and down her inner thighs and up to her rather small breasts.

Once the song ended, she stayed in his lap, sipping her vodka drink. Hunter needed no more convincing that she was going to be his girl tonight, and apparently, she had taken a liking to him as well.

She whispered in his ear, "You want sexo?"

He hadn't planned on paying for sex tonight, but then again, he hadn't ruled it out either. The bottom line was that he couldn't tell this girl no. "How much?" he inquired.

"For you, ciento."

Hunter didn't think this was much of a discount on the going rate, but he couldn't find it in himself to say no. "Alright, you talked me into it. Let's get another round of drinks first."

Hunter got up, grabbed her hand, and walked around the table to where Cinco was still playing with Maria, one dollar at a time. "Man, I'm going to need you to spot me seventy-five." He was slightly embarrassed to ask for money in front of Veronica, but he didn't think she would care too much where the money was coming from.

Cinco looked up with a huge drunken grin on his face and reached for his wallet. "Have fun, brother," he said, handing Hunter the seventy-five dollars.

After their trip to the bar, Veronica led him by the hand to her room in back. The rooms were set up like any other hotel, and when she got to hers, she unlocked it with a key that she kept somewhere in her bustier. They entered the room, and Hunter was somewhat surprised by its college dorm room–like appearance. There were a couple of pictures of people who were probably family, a few posters, and a stuffed animal. Veronica pushed him to sit down on the bed. She lay a sleeve of condoms from her nightstand on the bed next to him.

Hunter sipped his beer while she took off her bustier, revealing perfect, teardrop-shaped tits. She took one last drink of her cocktail and sat down next to him. She took his beer and hat and helped him get his clothes off. Hunter was sure he had the look of a kid in a candy store on his face as she gently pushed him back down onto the bed. They were silent except for occasional laughter to make up for the moments of awkwardness.

Over an hour later, Hunter and Veronica returned to the bar. He bought her another drink, kissed her good-bye, and went back to the table, where Maria was still dancing for Cinco. They'd moved on from beers to whiskey. Hunter sat down and took off his hat, revealing his soaking wet hair. Cinco started laughing. "Hey, bud, were you back there working that hard, or did you get a shower?"

Hunter looked at him with a straight face. "Man, we needed a shower."

Cinco laughed hysterically. When he caught his breath, he said, "Do you have a few bucks left on you? Ms. Maria here has taken all my cash."

Hunter pulled out his last ten dollars and handed it across the table. Cinco slid the ten into the front side of Maria's panties, kissed her on the cheek, and, in very slurred speech, thanked her for the dances.

"Thank you. It was fun." She picked up her bra and headed back behind the stage.

Cinco looked over at Hunter with a frustrated look on his face, "I hope she was good, bud. I took one for the team tonight."

Hunter smiled slyly at that comment. "She was awesome, and you're fixin' to be a married man." The last part of that was not absent of some cynicism. *She should have paid me*, he thought to himself. *I went for forty-five minutes, and she came twice.*

"Well, bud, we're out of cash, I'm fucked up, and I think you've done all the damage you're gonna do this evening." Cinco carefully got up from his chair. "Vámonos." He sauntered toward the front door.

"Shit, I guess it's time to go," Hunter muttered and pounded what was left of his Modelo Especial.

Just as Cinco was reaching for the door, a half-dozen soldiers in black urban assault gear, faces covered with black ski masks underneath black helmets, and with their weapons drawn, came bounding into the front of the bar.

"Holy shit!" Hunter felt a sobering sense of alarm come over him as he instinctively raised both hands in the air. He was far enough removed from the door not to come face-to-face with one of the paramilitaries, but Cinco wasn't so lucky. He looked in horror as the lead man through the door had Cinco facedown against the bar, arms pinned behind him, with some kind of submachine gun pressed to the back of his head. Hunter couldn't quite make out what was being said through all the yelling and commotion, but it was clear the other soldiers were not interested in him as they ran right by. Hunter's attention was focused solely on Cinco and what was happening to his best friend.

After what seemed like an eternity but was probably less than a minute, the soldier pinning down Cinco let him up and moved toward the back of the bar with the rest of his comrades. Whatever or whoever they were looking for didn't include two drunk gringos. Hunter breathed a sigh of relief as he realized that they were going to make it out of Hunter's Ranch alive. He made eye contact with Cinco, and they quietly stepped to the door and exited the bar as inconspicuously as was humanly possible.

Once they were in the parking lot, their cautious movement gave way to a dead sprint to the truck. Hunter hadn't heard any shots fired, but he didn't want to stick around to find out what was going on. He fired up the truck without saying a word, put it in reverse, and mashed his foot down on the gas pedal a little more aggressively than he had intended. The gravel went flying as he threw the truck in drive before it had stopped reversing.

Several minutes went by before either of them could speak. Hunter remained focused on the road, trying to process all that had just occurred.

"Man, all I could think about was that I didn't want Mia to hear that I died in a Mexican whorehouse." Cinco, clearly rattled but equally drunk, was holding his head in his hands.

"What did he say to you?"

Cinco looked up. "He asked, 'Who the fuck are you?' in Spanish, and I told him three times before he finally told us to get out of there."

"Who were those guys?"

"Fuck if I know," Cinco said. "Some kind of Mexican special forces." He put his head back in his hands. "We're never going to talk about this."

Hunter nodded in acknowledgment and honored his best friend's request by staying silent.

The ride back to the border was much less eventful than the trip to Boy's Town. It was almost three in the morning by the time they made their way back to Calle Madero, the one-way street leading to the border crossing.

Hunter commented on how they hadn't seen a soul in town, not even la policía, and then decided to end his several-week sabbatical from the Copenhagen. Eighteen hours of drinking, forty-five minutes of sex, and ninety seconds of life-threatening chaos had taken their toll on him, and he needed to stay alert to get back to the ranch. The last image of Acuña he had that morning was the same as the one that had greeted them the previous evening: the armored personnel carrier with the kid manning a fifty-caliber machine gun. He wondered whether the man who had held the gun to the back of Cinco's head was as young as this one appeared to be. The itchy trigger finger of a kid in a soldier's uniform could have resulted in the loss of yet another friend.

He looked over at Cinco, who was passed out in the passenger's seat, and said, "This was the last hurrah in Old Mexico, bud. Times have definitely changed."

As they slowly approached the US Customs checkpoint across the bridge, Hunter shook Cinco's shoulder in an attempt to wake him up. The driver's side window was already rolled down, and the customs agent stuck his head nearly inside, looking at Cinco. "Is he okay?" the agent asked.

"Yes, sir," Hunter said. "Just a little overserved tonight. He'll be fine."

The agent took a hard look at Hunter. "What about you? Were you overserved as well?"

"No, sir. I'm the DD tonight," Hunter said with a straight face.

He knew he wasn't convincing anybody that he hadn't been drinking, but customs had never been too concerned about drinking and driving.

"You're both US citizens?"

"Yes, sir."

"You bringing anything out of Mexico?"

"No, sir."

"You know Mexico is not a safe place to be at three in the morning, right?"

Hunter looked the agent straight in the eyes and paused as if he wanted to say more. "Yes, sir."

"Well, get home safe."

Once they were through customs, Hunter cranked up the volume on the stereo to Steve Earle's "The Week of Living Dangerously," which perfectly summed up the night. He kept the truck at a speed that was slightly lower than the limit and focused on getting them home in one piece. It had been a crazy night in Mexico, kind of fitting for what he knew would be the last trip in a long while. If Alfredo knew what he was talking about, the border was about to turn into a bigger war zone than it already was. The increased military presence and the apparent raid at Hunter's Ranch had been a pretty good indication of what was yet to come. Acuña had completely lost the safe and casual atmosphere that it had always been known for.

His thoughts drifted to Veronica and that gorgeous body that he'd had full access to earlier in the evening. Then, as they typically did after long nights of drinking, his thoughts quickly turned to Beth and then to Ty. The alcohol was still covering the anxiety, but the feeling of loneliness was creeping in. Songs always triggered

memories for Hunter, and Steve Earle's "Ben McCulloch" was one
of Ty's favorites. Hunter knew the words by heart and sang loudly
with the stereo in an attempt to not focus on his thoughts as he
passed through downtown Del Rio.

It was after 4:00 a.m. when Hunter pulled the truck into the
circular drive at the F bar R. Cinco woke up as Hunter was getting
out of the truck.

"Let's go, man. We're home," was all Hunter had the energy to
say. He waited for Cinco to climb out of the truck and then locked
it up.

He had noticed Stacy's Suburban in the drive in front of the
main headquarters, and instead of feeling the awkward embarrassment from that afternoon for not calling her, he actually wanted
to see her, hoping that by some chance she might be still awake,
waiting for them in the hunting lodge. It might have only been that
the conversation would be easier drunk, but he thought that there
could be more to it than that.

His hopes were dashed as he and Cinco stumbled into the dark
and empty lodge and made their way to their room. After a bottle of
water and some eight-hundred-milligram Motrin, it was finally time
to call it a night. Cinco, who hadn't said anything since they crossed
the border, pulled off his boots and said, "Good run tonight, bud."

Hunter snorted and smirked. "You know it, brother. Ty would
have been proud."

CHAPTER 6

STACY

Hunter woke up three hours later. The sun was flooding into their room, and there was no going back to sleep. He found himself analyzing the events of the night before, wondering who those guys were and what they were looking for, imagining himself and Cinco being caught in crossfire. Aware that the cartels prevented media from reporting anything along the border, he searched the Internet on his phone for answers to questions he knew he would never find.

Being hungover only made his ruminating and anxiety worse, so he made himself get up. The Motrin had worked to mitigate a headache, but the other effects of dysphoria and lethargy were painfully present. He moved carefully, so as not to wake up Cinco in the other set of bunks, grabbed a change of clothes, and made his way to the shower. The hot water, which was considerably hotter than the shower he had the night before in Boy's Town, helped relax his mind and aching body.

Once he was out of the shower, he put on a clean pair of jeans, a long-sleeve T-shirt, his camo fleece vest, and his ranch boots to step out into the lodge's great room. Someone had been kind enough to start a pot of coffee, and he helped himself by filling a Styrofoam cup to the brim. Caffeine would at least help with the lethargic effects of the hangover. The next remedy would be fresh air, and he decided he would move out to the back patio to enjoy his coffee and take in the Devils River scenery.

He got about five feet from the door when he realized who had made the coffee. Sitting in the same chair he had been sitting in when he and Cinco were drinking beer the previous afternoon, with a cup of coffee in one hand and a novel in the other, was Stacy Sanderson, Ty's little sister.

"Son of a bitch," he muttered under his breath. The desire to see her from earlier in the morning had turned to sheer terror of an awkward situation. He knew there was nothing he could do but walk out there and face her, but part of him wanted to crawl back in bed to delay the inevitable. He took a deep breath and quietly opened the French doors to the patio. Stacy had her back turned to the doors and didn't hear him come outside.

"Good morning, Stace," he said.

Stacy put her book down, pushed her stylish sunglasses up on top of her head, and looked Hunter up and down. "Mornin' sunshine. I tried to wait up for y'all last night, but I gave up at two. You look like shit, and that says a lot coming from me." She was known for her ability to hold her own on an all-night bender.

Hunter put his Costa Del Mars on to block out some of the light, sat down, and looked over at her. "Thanks, I feel pretty good too."

Although Hunter clearly didn't look his best, he thought she had never looked better. It was never a lack of attraction that had kept him from pursuing Stacy, who he knew had been passively pursuing him for years. He had always found her long, black hair and crystal-clear blue eyes to be extremely striking. Her nearly five-foot-eleven-inch athletic frame had contributed to her high school success in volleyball and had also opened the door to some modeling opportunities in college. The bottom line was that he had always thought she was hot, but in high school, she was Ty's little sister, and he was with Beth. Their paths rarely crossed in college because by the time she was in Fort Worth at TCU, Ty had already left Austin to fight the Taliban, and Hunter didn't see as much of their family.

This morning, she wore no makeup. Her hair was pulled back into a ponytail, and she was wearing an old pair of designer jeans over her scuffed-up ranch boots and a tight-fitting sweater that revealed the shape of her well-proportioned breasts. It was the perfect combination of sexy and ranch style, and Hunter knew it was intentional.

"Stace, I'm—"

"I'm not." She had a stern look on her face. "We're all hurting right now."

The response caught Hunter completely off guard.

"There's nothing to be sorry about," she said. "This weekend is about Ty, and he would probably be pissed at both of us." She managed to laugh in lieu of crying, which Hunter could tell was difficult.

"You really think he would be pissed?" Hunter asked, with a sarcastic smile on his face.

"You got drunk with his little sister and had sex with her. I'm pretty sure he would have kicked your ass!"

They both laughed and began comparing notes from the night

they had spent together, which neither of them remembered entirely. Then Stacy got serious. "I've got a little bit of bad news."

Hunter couldn't imagine a scenario that would make him mad at Stacy after she had lifted such a huge weight off of his mind. She had that girlish look on her face like she didn't want to tell him something.

"Tell me you're not pregnant." It was the only thing he could come up with.

She laughed. "No! Nothing like that."

Hunter breathed a sigh of relief. "Okay, what is it?"

She was cowering as if she thought Hunter was going to lash out at her. "You know I was living with my parents when Ty died, right? Well, when I got home that next morning after the service, my parents asked me where I had been all night. I kind of told them that I stayed at your place."

This was a scenario that hadn't occurred to Hunter. "Holy shit! You didn't!"

"Yeah, I did," she said, sheepishly.

Hunter took a second to process what she had revealed to him. "You do know that I'm fixin' to spend a whole weekend climbing a mountain with your dad, right?"

She was making a weak effort not to laugh. "Well, he doesn't know what happened, only that I was too drunk to drive, so I stayed at your place."

"Oh, that makes it better," he said. "When I don't come back from West Texas, it's gonna be your fault."

Stacy sneered. "You know he thinks of you as a second son. He's not going to kill you."

Hunter looked at her like she was out of her mind. "Well, he's definitely not going to be too happy about it. You're his only daughter." He downed the rest of his coffee. "I'm so fucked."

She laughed uncontrollably as he continued to give her a serious, inquisitive look.

"Would you like another cup of coffee?" he asked. He wanted to be alone for a minute.

"Yes, sir," she said. "That would be nice. Thank you."

He got up slowly from his chair and walked back into the lodge, wondering whether she may have caught on to the fact that he was struggling with depression and that was why she was being so cool about him not calling her. Or maybe she was just naturally that cool. Either way, her seemingly carefree attitude and dry sense of humor put him a little more at ease about the whole situation. He found himself actually wanting to spend more time with her on the porch.

Minutes later, Hunter returned with two full cups of coffee. Stacy, who had put her sunglasses back on and was staring west out over the river, thanked him and handled the cup with both hands to warm them up. It was a beautiful morning, with very few clouds in the sky, but there was still a chill in the January air. Hunter sat down and silently shared the view with her.

After several minutes, he broke the silence. "Did you ever make this trip with your dad and Ty?"

Stacy shifted her gaze back to him. "No, this was always a boys' trip. My mom and I would either hang out here or go to the spa in SA. I always wanted to, though. The way they talked about it made it sound amazing. The closest they had ever been to heaven."

"That's exactly how Ty would describe it." Hunter smiled fondly. "How are Jess and Junior?"

Stacy shrugged. "They're here, but it's been tough. I've spent most of my free time with them. Ty is getting big."

"I can't believe he's three months old." Hunter felt terrible that he hadn't been by to see his godson.

Stacy got up from her chair and gestured for him to follow her. "Let's go see him. My mom has breakfast going, and I'm sure Jess and Ty are up by now."

Stacy led him over to the massive headquarters via a tile walkway connecting the two patios. The back patio area of the headquarters was even more grandiose than the lodge's. A huge covered pavilion sat on the edge of the cliff overlooking the river. Under the tin roof of the pavilion was a full outdoor kitchen and bar on one side, a large dining table in the middle, and a massive rock outdoor fireplace on the other side, surrounded by rocking chairs. Hunter recalled many occasions when he and Ty had sat in those rocking chairs, solving the world's problems one drink at a time.

The walkway led to wide-open French doors and the distinct smell of bacon frying on a skillet. Stacy had been right; both Jessica and Ty Junior were at the breakfast table inside. The site of Jessica holding her son and feeding him with a bottle nearly brought Hunter to tears before he even stepped foot in the house. Jessica, with her blond, curly hair and big blue eyes, had always been beautiful, but this morning, she looked stressed and tired, and Hunter felt terrible that he hadn't helped her over the last month.

"Look who I found out and about!" Stacy said as they walked in together.

Jessica looked up from the baby and smiled at Hunter. "Hey! I'd get up to give you a hug, but he's pretty hungry."

Martha Sanderson, Ty and Stacy's mom, adjusted one of the

burners on the stove and then walked over. "Hunter Sharp, you get over here and give me a hug." It was very clear that Stacy and Ty both got their height from their dad, because Martha was absolutely tiny. Hunter's eyes welled up as he tightly embraced Mrs. Sanderson. "You know it means so much to Michael that y'all are doing this," she said.

Hunter wondered whether Dr. Sanderson would truly be appreciative of his presence on the trip, knowing that Stacy had spent the night at his house. He wiped his eyes as he sat down at the table next to Jessica. "How's this big guy doing?"

"He's good. Just missing his godfather."

Hunter gently rubbed the top of baby Ty's head, which was full of fuzzy blond hair. "I know, Jess. Sorry I haven't been around much lately."

"The holidays are always tough." She smiled. "I know how to find you."

Stacy, who had been working on something in the kitchen with her mom, returned to the table holding two plates with omelets, bacon, and fresh fruit. She put one of the plates in front of Hunter and sat down next to him. He thanked Martha for making breakfast and picked away at his food. His stomach was doing better after the coffee, but it was still a little uneasy. The greasy bacon, which he devoured, would certainly help with the hangover. As he took his second bite, Cinco came walking down the outside walkway toward the French doors. He had showered and changed into a clean pair of jeans and starched short-sleeve shirt, but there was no hiding how he felt physically.

Stacy laughed as he walked into the room. "Look what the cat dragged in," she said. "Good morning, Cinco."

Cinco removed his Costa Del Mars and faked a smile. "Mornin' Stace, Jess, Mrs. Sanderson."

"Y'all must have had a big time last night!" Martha handed him a cup of coffee and gave him a hug.

Cinco gave Hunter the *don't say a word* look as he took a sip of coffee.

"Sit down," Martha said, "and I'll get you some breakfast. Michael called not too long ago from Houston. They should be here in an hour or so."

The plan was for Dr. Sanderson to fly his plane from San Antonio to Houston to pick up Chris James, a fraternity brother of theirs from the Houston area, and Jack Nelson, who lived in Dallas but would meet the plane in Houston. They got the luxury of a three-hour flight to the ranch instead of a six-hour drive.

Stacy mentioned that she hadn't seen Cinco or Mia since Ty's services and had only heard through the grapevine that they had got engaged. She clearly wanted to hear all about it, and Cinco could barely keep his food down, which Hunter found extremely entertaining. It was painfully obvious how hungover Cinco was, but Stacy kept on peppering him with questions. They had known each other all of their lives and often acted like siblings. She clearly knew how to irritate him and was doing a fine job of it this morning.

Martha placed Cinco's plate on the table. "He doesn't feel good, Stacy," she said. "Let the boy eat."

"Thanks, Mrs. Sanderson," Cinco said, and gave her a smile of gratitude. He glared at Stacy.

Once Cinco finished his breakfast, Stacy suggested that the two "boys" follow Jessica and her to the airstrip to wait for her dad and their friends. She would take one of the ranch Jeeps, and they could follow in Cinco's truck. Martha agreed to watch baby Ty to let Jessica get a much-needed break. The four of them walked out to the four-car garage attached to the headquarters, which housed two Jeep Wranglers with elevated backseats and Cole's old pickup that had been turned into a quail rig in the back, dog kennels and all.

Stacy pushed the automatic garage door opener and grabbed a Yeti cooler out of the back of the cleaner-looking Jeep. She loaded the cooler with Miller Lights, her beer of choice, and ice from the garage refrigerator. With a mischievous grin, she looked at Hunter and Cinco and asked, "A little hair of the dog, boys?"

Hunter was amused by her humor. "Yes, ma'am. I like your style." He grabbed a couple of beers and followed Cinco out to his truck as Stacy started the Jeep and drove out of the garage.

The drive to the airstrip took only about five minutes, but it was long enough for Cinco to harass Hunter about Stacy and ask about their coffee conversation. Hunter made every effort not to act defensive and replied that he and Stacy had a good talk and things were "cool," even though he was still trying to wrap his head around how cool things were. They followed Stacy as she pulled her Jeep in front of the small hangar Dr. Sanderson had erected for his airplane. She turned up the volume of the XM satellite radio she had tuned to a nineties pop station and climbed up on the hood of the Jeep, where she sat cross-legged. Jessica joined her on the Jeep as Cinco backed his truck up next to them. He and Hunter dropped the tailgate on the pickup and took a seat to watch the plane come in.

A stiff, cool breeze out of the north blew the big orange windsock at the north end of the flight line back toward their position on the south end. Although the breeze was cool, the morning chill had given way to a warm rising sun, and the temperature had become very pleasant. It was the kind of winter day in Southwest Texas where it felt good to be outside, and it certainly made dealing with a hangover easier.

Hunter had finished his beer by the time they lowered the tailgate, and he was reaching for another from the Jeep when Stacy sassed, "Whoa, killer! You better not drink all of my beer!"

He laughed. "You better keep up! I came to party."

Stacy's facial expression turned serious. "Don't mess with me, Hunter," she said. "I'll drink you under the table."

"I have no doubt." Hunter opened a fresh Miller Light and sat next to Cinco on the tailgate. Jessica looked inquisitively at Cinco, who shook his head.

About twenty minutes later, the single-engine Cessna 172S Skyhawk showed up on the horizon. Dr. Sanderson did one flyby of the airstrip before he came back around for his landing from the south. The airplane was a 2008 model that Dr. Sanderson had purchased a year ago from a colleague who upgraded to a bigger plane. Ty had told Hunter all about the new plane, which he and his dad had flown out to Big Bend only a year earlier. Ty, like his father, loved flying and was an instrument-rated pilot.

The approach and landing seemed to take forever as the slow-moving Cessna made its final descent onto the asphalt runway. It touched down only a few yards from the group waiting for it on the ground. The burnt-orange longhorn emblem on the tail made both Hunter and Cinco smile. They all got up from their seats to greet the plane and its crew as it sped past them toward the north end of the runway and turned around to taxi back to the south. The plane shut down feet from where they were parked, and Stacy was the first to greet her dad as he swung open the single door on the pilot's side. Dr. Michael Sanderson, tall and lanky, like both Ty and Stacy, somehow managed to unfold from the cockpit and stepped out onto the asphalt tarmac to give his daughter a long embrace. He looked like the perfect combination of rancher and pilot with his F bar R baseball cap, aviator sunglasses, faded blue jeans, and roper-style work boots.

Following Dr. Sanderson, and exiting the aircraft from the copilot seat, was a medium-height, slightly overweight guy sporting a light-brown, unkempt full beard, wearing Wrangler blue jeans, an untucked button-down short-sleeve shirt, and a camouflage baseball cap. Hunter was particularly looking forward to catching up with Chris James, whom he hadn't spent time with, other than at Ty's service, since Chris's wedding over a year ago. They had been roommates in college their junior year and remained good friends.

Chris was a native Houstonian who, with his naturally laid-back demeanor, seemed to be a better fit in Austin. His carefree approach to life served as a comforting balance to Hunter's anxiety and worries. They also shared a love of live music, and it was Chris who had introduced Hunter to the far-too-enjoyable experience of smoking pot prior to attending shows by popular jam bands such as Widespread Panic or Phish. A talented musician himself, Chris always had a guitar in hand and would pick out songs at parties and late-night get-togethers.

Graduating from Texas with an English major, he got into writing and was now working for an Austin-based publishing company as an editor. It was work he could do from anywhere. When he married a fellow Houstonian, Sarah Bradley, who owned a successful clothing store located in Houston, the year before, he reluctantly moved back home. They recently had their first child, a little girl named Sloan. It was extremely difficult for Hunter to picture Chris as a dad, but his friend definitely had the patience for it.

Jack Nelson was the last passenger out the door of the Cessna. Jack stood about five foot nine and weighed 150 pounds soaking wet. His curly blond hair was a little longer than that of any of the other guys in the group, and his dress a little more Dallas than West Texas, with his Ralph Lauren Polo shirt, North Face fleece vest, and Dallas Country Club baseball cap.

Originally from Austin but now living in the fast lane in Dallas, Jack was the son of a US senator and had always seemed to Hunter to be trying his damnedest to prove that he was anything but like his father. He was the consummate cut-up, and trouble always seemed to find him, something his family must have discovered early in his life when they made the decision to send him away to a Virginia-based boarding school. After returning to Austin for college, which he stretched out an extra year and a half, he took a sales job in Dallas and had managed to sustain his party lifestyle ever since. Hunter supposed Jack had no problem keeping up with the Joneses in Dallas, because he always seemed to have unlimited funding, a virtue that they had all benefited from at one point or another during their college years.

Chris and Jack, though good friends, were the antithesis of each other. Initial first impressions of them standing together, which were unsurprisingly accurate, conjured thoughts of a remarkable clash of cultures: preppy, big-city playboy meets East Texas pot-smoking hippie. The contradictions didn't stop with appearance. Chris was a man of few words, whereas Jack was a gregarious storyteller, "full of shit" being the descriptive phrase most commonly used by those closest to him. It wasn't hard to tell whom Hunter identified with more, but college was a beautiful thing, in that it brought guys together who may not have otherwise been buddies.

Hunter and Cinco remained sitting on the tailgate of the truck, sipping their beers, as Dr. Sanderson opened the baggage compartment for his two passengers and started his postflight inspection of his plane. Both Chris and Jack retrieved a bag from the little compartment behind the cockpit and made their way toward the parked vehicles.

Chris said hi to Jessica, then turned toward his buddies, and, in his soft-spoken, slow dialect, matter-of-factly stated, "You boys don't get up. We're good."

Cinco didn't move an inch, but Hunter extended his hand to shake both Chris's and Jack's. "Y'all missed a big time last night in Old Mexico."

Jack threw his bag into the bed of the truck and sarcastically replied, "I'm glad y'all made it back alive."

The irony of the comment was not lost on Hunter, and he could see the same look on Cinco's face as well.

"You have a cocktail for us?" Jack asked. "I had a rough one in H-town last night."

Hunter pointed Jack to the Jeep and then shifted his attention back to the plane, where Dr. Sanderson was unloading a small cedar chest. He knew the chest contained Ty's ashes. He stood up as if at attention in a military tribute. Cinco, Jessica, and the other two followed suit, halting conversation to watch Dr. Sanderson carry his son's ashes toward them. Chris put his arm around Jessica, who had begun sobbing.

Dr. Sanderson walked briskly toward the two vehicles, a duffel bag slung over one shoulder and the cedar chest in both hands.

Stacy was by his side. He handed the cedar chest to Jessica. Tears streaked down her face from underneath her sunglasses. He gave her a long hug. To Hunter's surprise, Ty's dad turned to him next and extended his hand.

"Hunter, good to see you, son." His facial expression was stern, and his voice was void of emotion, indications to Hunter that he may not really have been happy to see him.

"Yes, sir. Good to see you, too." Hunter maintained his composure, despite feeling an overwhelming sense of anxiety throughout the awkwardly long and firm handshake. Once her dad moved on to greet Cinco, Stacy's eyes, though hidden by sunglasses, met Hunter's, and she broke into a nervous smile. He shook his head ever so slightly at her, still in angst over the fact that her dad knew they had spent the night together.

Five minutes later, Dr. Sanderson was in the driver's seat of the Jeep, accompanied by Stacy in the backseat and Jessica sitting shotgun, turning off of the asphalt runway onto the dirt road toward the headquarters. Cinco closed the tailgate of his truck and started the engine while Chris and Jack loaded up in the backseat. Chris, despite being a fraternity brother of Ty's for the limited amount of time Ty was in Austin, was the only one of the group who had not been to the ranch.

Hunter looked back from his front seat and welcomed him to the F bar R. "Man, I can't believe you've never been out here before."

Chris had his window down to fully appreciate the beauty of both the ranch and the picture-perfect January weather. He smiled. "I know. I wish I would have taken Ty up on one of those midnight runs freshman year."

Ty's "midnight runs" to the ranch from Austin after fraternity parties had become legendary their freshman year in college. He would take as many as he could talk into going and that could fit into his crew-cab pickup, girls receiving immediate priority over guys.

Jack held his beer out for a toast. He was never one to turn down a party, and he'd made several trips out to the ranch with Ty during his college years.

"Cheers, boys," he said. "It's good to be here. Here's to Ty."

They raised their beers to acknowledge the toast.

"Salud, brother." Cinco looked in his rearview mirror at Chris and Jack in the backseat. "This might be the last trip out to the F bar R. It's been about twenty years' worth of good times. I think our first trip out here was for Ty's birthday when we were probably eight or nine."

Cinco was the only one in the truck who had been friends with Ty since birth. They had grown up together in San Antonio. He then turned his gaze toward Hunter and smirked. "Hunter's our last shot at coming back. He's got to seal the deal."

Chris looked at Hunter with apparent disbelief. "With Ty's sister? That girl is way too hot for you, Sharp. The man has been gone for less than a month, and you're already after his sister?"

Cinco laughed. "She's after him. Has been for years. I don't get it either!"

Hunter finished what was left of his beer and, in lieu of coming across as defensive, decided not to respond. He glared at Cinco through his green-mirrored sunglasses.

"Holy shit, this place is awesome," Chris said flatly, displaying about as much enthusiasm as he ever did. He was extremely laid back and less excitable than anyone Hunter had ever met.

As Cinco pulled the pickup up in front of the headquarters,

Hunter looked back at his old roommate. "Wait 'til you see the view of the river from the back."

The four of them unloaded from the truck, and Hunter led the way between the headquarters and the lodge to the huge pavilion on the edge of the cliff. They took seats in the rocking chairs set up around the massive rock fireplace.

Martha Sanderson was right behind them, coming out of the house to greet the two newcomers. "Jack, how are ya?"

Jack jumped up from his rocking chair and hugged her. "I'm good, Martha. Good to see you." She asked about his family, to which he shortly replied, "They're all good."

"Martha, do you remember Chris?" Hunter asked.

She smiled and, whether she remembered him or not, gave the appearance that she knew him well. "Chris, welcome to the ranch."

"Thank you for having us out," he said and gave her a hug. "This is a beautiful place."

"Thank you. There's cold beer in the fridge under the bar there, and we're going to feed y'all before you get on the road, so make yourselves at home."

They responded nearly in unison with four yes ma'ams as she walked back into the house.

Hunter was the first one to the fridge, and he quickly passed beers to the other three, who all seemed to be mesmerized by the view of the Devils River flowing along the base of the cliff, more than a hundred feet below. The wind was still strong out of the north, steadily pushing the south-flowing water.

"We've got to come back in the spring and do one of those canoe trips down the river," Cinco remarked, not directly talking to anyone. "You camp out and fish all the way down to Amistad. It's a good opportunity to break out a fly rod."

Hunter knew Cinco was the most skilled with a fly rod of the group. As a kid, he had spent summers in Montana fly-fishing with his dad. Cinco had actually taught Hunter, who had always used spinning tackle, how to throw a fly at redfish on the Lower Laguna Madre when they were in high school. Hunter thought it was funny that fly-fishing had developed an almost cult-like following among young anglers across the country. The "cult" had developed its own subculture, which many of the old-time plugging fishing guides viewed as just plain weird. Fly fisherman were purists. They had their own gear, tied their own flies, and would rather spend hours stalking one fish than catching a lot of fish by more conventional means. Watching that first redfish eat a fly had Hunter hooked, figuratively speaking, on the sport.

It wasn't long until Martha, followed by Dr. Sanderson and Cole, came back out to the pavilion, carrying a large pan. She set the pan on the bar next to the outdoor kitchen and announced that her husband was making burgers for everyone prior to their trip. Cole introduced himself to Chris and then took a seat at the table. Dr. Sanderson explained that they had a lot of hamburger in their freezer from the steer they had slaughtered last spring. He was working away on the grill when Stacy and Jessica came into the pavilion.

"Where's that baby boy?" Jack asked Jessica. "I'm sure he's grown a lot in a month."

Jessica pointed to the little monitor clipped to her belt. "He's sleeping. Apparently, he's got his days and nights mixed up, because he didn't want to sleep last night."

"He's going to be a night owl like his daddy," Jack said.

The comment sent the group into an awkward silence, and Jessica stared west across the river through her sunglasses, obviously avoiding eye contact with anyone and trying to not break down in tears.

"So have any of y'all been up to San Isabel Peak before?" Martha asked from behind the bar. San Isabel was the favorite peak of Ty's and Dr. Sanderson's in Big Bend National Park and the planned destination for the trip.

Cinco, taking a visual cue from the other three, answered that no, none of them had been up on that particular peak. He explained that he was the only one of the group who had even been out to the park.

Chris mentioned that he had been out to a friend's ranch just north of the park for a quail hunt, but he had never done any hiking in the park itself.

"Boys, I hope you brought your hiking boots," Dr. Sanderson said. "The hike is no walk in the park." He had emailed them a list of things to bring, but Hunter, who didn't own a pair of hiking boots, had brought only running shoes. He wasn't too worried. How bad could it be? He was in decent shape, and mountains in Texas couldn't be that high.

The smell of the hamburgers cooking on the grill made everyone hungry, particularly the two fighting bad hangovers. The couple of beers had really helped Hunter get to a stable state, but he could tell Cinco was still struggling. He had been quiet all morning, a definite indication that he wasn't feeling well. Hunter would typically give him a hard time about it, but he decided not to in front of Ty's parents.

"Anybody need another cerveza?" he asked. He was going to the refrigerator anyway. Everyone responded but Cinco, who was still sipping his beer.

"Cinco, are you okay over there?" Stacy asked. "What's wrong—you can't hang?"

Hunter laughed out loud on his way to the bar and retrieved five beers to distribute to the group.

Lunch was served after Martha led the group in prayer. Hunter intentionally sat on the opposite side of the table from Stacy, overly conscious of Dr. Sanderson's watchful eyes. The burgers, served medium-well and flavored with fajita seasoning, were well received by all, especially Cinco, who nearly inhaled his food.

"That is exactly what I needed," he said, leaning back in his chair, appearing a little more at ease. "If I could take a little siesta, I'd be money."

Dr. Sanderson got up from the table. "You're going to have to take that siesta on the road," he said. "We better get going if we want to get there by dark."

Hunter turned to Cinco and offered to drive. He knew he wouldn't be able to fall asleep on the road because he couldn't ever sleep through a hangover. It was like his brain was programmed to punish him every time he drank too much. And, inevitably, his ruminations and anxiety would intensify as he lay awake. His philosophy was that he either had to suffer through the hangover or delay the inevitable suffering by drinking it away. Often the best option seemed to be staying drunk.

Everyone thanked the Sandersons for the lunch, and Martha cleared the table as her husband made his way back into the house. Jessica also excused herself from the table to check on baby Ty.

Cinco reached into his shirt pocket and retrieved his can of Copenhagen snuff, packed it with a flick of his index finger, opened the can, grabbed a sizeable pinch of the finely cut tobacco, and put it inside his lip. Chris nodded to indicate that he wanted a dip. Cinco threw the can across the table to him, and Chris went through the same routine. Cole followed suit, pulling his own can from the back pocket of his blue jeans.

Hunter ran his fingers through his thinning brown hair and thought about having another beer. He wanted to be careful to maintain that stable state, where he was feeling good but not so good that he wouldn't be able to drive for the three to four hours it would take them to get to the park. Instead, he decided he should get ready to go.

"I'm going to pack up the truck. I'll grab your bag," he offered to Cinco.

"You're a good man." Cinco tossed the keys to his truck to Hunter. "I don't care what Stacy says about you."

Stacy smirked smartly at Cinco and followed Hunter down the Saltillo walkway to the lodge.

"You need some help?"

She was obviously looking for a reason to come along. "No, ma'am, but I'll take the company." He turned around to let her catch up, and they walked into the lodge together.

The four others watched them until they disappeared into the house. "Sharp's going to hit that!" Jack said. Cinco smiled like he knew something the other three didn't. The look on Cole's face was one of awkwardness. He was clearly uncomfortable with the idea of Stacy being romantically involved with anyone. The banter continued, despite his lack of participation, for several minutes until the conversation finally changed to embellished stories about big deer they had seen over the years.

In the room he'd stayed in, Hunter packed his bag while Stacy sat on the opposite bed, where Cinco had slept, a beer in her hand.

"See, I told you my dad wasn't going to kill you." She smiled.

He stopped packing. "The weekend is young. Did you see the way he was looking at me?"

That brought a laugh. "You're just paranoid."

"What does your mom want us to do with these sheets?" He shook the pillow out of its case.

"Strip them, and leave them on the floor." Stacy set her beer on the nightstand and began tugging the sheets off of the bed she had been sitting on. "We have a maid who comes out on Monday."

Hunter followed her directions and picked up his bag, his gun case, and Cinco's bag. "We better get loaded up."

He knew it was obvious he was a little anxious about being in the lodge alone with Stacy with her parents next door. Very much unlike her, Stacy must have decided not to give him too hard of a time about it.

Out front, Dr. Sanderson was loading his gear into Stacy's white Suburban. As he glanced at Hunter and Stacy walking out, they instinctively parted ways, as if exiting the lodge at the same time had been a coincidence. Hunter loaded the bags into Cinco's Chevy while Stacy attended to her dad to see whether she could help him. Once the bags were loaded up, Hunter's attention turned to the cedar chest containing Ty's ashes, which was lying in the cargo area of the Suburban. What was left of his friend would be making the trip to West Texas with them.

The rest of the crew made their way toward the front of the

headquarters, loudly telling stories, most of which Hunter was pretty sure were only half true. Cole loaded a duffel bag into the back of the Suburban as the others gathered around the two vehicles. Dr. Sanderson handed a professional-looking Nikon camera to Stacy and asked for the group to get together for a picture. The six of them responded slowly, assembling into a gaggle in front of the Suburban.

Jack, the last to get in line, looked at the other five and smirked. "Better get it now, while we're all still alive."

"You planning on not making it back from this one, bud?" Hunter asked.

"Nelson, you better get ready," Cinco said. "Things are fixin' to get real western around here. Don't know if a Dallas boy can handle it."

Jack grinned. "Time to saddle up, cowboy."

The picture turned out to be special, one of many that would permanently make each of their albums. The taller of the group, Hunter, Cole, and Dr. Sanderson, stood in the middle, leaning against the white Suburban with Jack, Chris, and Cinco on both ends, a little closer to the camera in almost a half-circle. Stacy took one black-and-white photo, which, with the hats and the boots, looked like it could have been from any era in Texas history if one ignored the Suburban and the modern-day sunglasses.

"Well, boys," Dr. Sanderson said. "Let's load up."

Hunter could sense the emotion in his voice. It was the first time Dr. Sanderson was taking the trip without his son. Stacy gave her dad a hug and told him to take care of her Suburban. Cole loaded up shotgun in the Suburban while Chris and Jack walked back to the Chevy pickup with Hunter and Cinco. Martha was standing on the front porch of the headquarters, tears rolling down her face, waving good-bye to the group. Hunter climbed up into the driver's seat of Cinco's truck and made eye contact with Stacy. She gave him a very inconspicuous wave, and he casually returned the gesture with the index and middle finger of his left hand, which was gripping the steering wheel.

Cinco, who planned for his siesta in the back, offered shotgun to Chris, who climbed up next to Hunter.

"We have any cold beers in this rig?" Chris asked.

Hunter shook his head. "Man, I think we drank it dry, but we'll have to make a pit stop at some point."

He plugged in his iPhone and hit shuffle. "Lone Star Hotel," a fitting Guy Clark tune, written in tribute to West Texas, came on. Hunter sang the words aloud and followed Dr. Sanderson east on the long dirt road out of the ranch.

CHAPTER 7

ABOUT A SIX-PACK

The only way to drive west from the ranch was to backtrack south into Del Rio and then turn northwest onto Highway 90. Neither Hunter nor Chris had ever been west of Del Rio, and both were clearly impressed by the Lake Amistad bridge, which crossed the highway. Looking west through the old trestle railway bridge that ran parallel to the highway, Hunter wondered where the lake's clear green water turned into Mexico.

"Boys, you haven't seen anything 'til you get to the Pecos River crossing," Cinco said.

The next twenty miles were somewhat subdued, as the lethargic effects of lunch and afternoon beers set in. Hunter found himself caught off guard by the sudden appearance of slow-speed warning signs and roadside safety cones on Highway 90. The Border Patrol checkpoint east of Comstock was nothing more than a mobile trailer parked on the side of the road.

"American citizens?"

It had only been about twelve hours since the last time Hunter had to answer this question. This time, it was one of two US Border Patrol agents, dressed in green fatigues, asking the question. Hunter watched in the side mirror as the second agent led a leashed German shepherd, sniffing away for contraband, around the back of the truck.

"Yes, sir," they all answered in unison.

"Where y'all headed?" The agent's tone had changed from official business to genuine curiosity, likely fueled by sheer boredom and loneliness. He couldn't have been any older than they were, and the monotony of his role in securing the nation's borders was clearly getting to him.

"Big Bend," Hunter said.

"Are you with the group in the Suburban?"

Hunter nodded his head. "Yes, sir. Going to say good-bye to a buddy."

The agent smiled. "Y'all be safe."

The town of Comstock, Texas, wasn't much to look at. There was an old café in a rock building at the Highway 163 intersection that didn't appear to be open, and only a couple of pickup trucks were parked outside the Comstock Motel, across the street. Hunter suspected that the trucks either belonged to deer hunters staying in town or Border Patrol agents, probably the only two things that kept the town alive. Two pumps stood outside an old metal filling station on the right-hand side of the road, but with no signage indicating that it was open or whether the old-style pumps actually worked. A half-dozen green-and-white Border Patrol vehicles were parked outside a building on the western edge of the town.

"This place is wild, man," Chris said, gaping as if he were a tourist in a foreign country.

The landscape began to change as they left Comstock. The brush was less sparse and less green, more of a sage color, and the terrain became increasingly rocky. The last sign of Comstock was an old mobile home on the left side of the highway. At the entrance to the driveway, a beat-up old marquee sign read, Deer Corn, Ammo, Cold Beer.

Hunter pointed it out to his passengers: "That's all you need to survive out here, bud."

Chris laughed. "The essentials. Who needs water?"

"It looks like water is hard to come by out here," Jack said. "Lord knows they don't get any rain. It's dry as a bone."

It was painfully clear that the drought had been extremely tough on this arid country.

"Not enough concrete for you, Nelson?" Chris didn't look back as he made the snide comment.

"I bet the night life is happening out here, man," Jack said, staring out the back window.

Dr. Sanderson had picked up the pace once they were outside of Comstock, and the two-vehicle caravan was now traveling at eighty miles an hour. As they approached a sign for Seminole Canyon State Park, the Suburban slowed down and signaled a left turn.

"Where are we going now?" Hunter thought aloud.

"We're at the Pecos, boys." Cinco must have woken up as the vehicle slowed down. "Welcome to West Texas, the last frontier."

They turned onto a poorly paved road and followed the signs to a Pecos River overlook. They pulled in behind Dr. Sanderson, alongside a couple of covered picnic tables.

The view wasn't immediately apparent from the road, but once they were out of their vehicles, the scenery was magnificent. The dark green river, while obviously low, was very impressive, flowing between the sheer rock walls of the canyon. The Highway 90 bridge, which could be seen to the north from their vantage point, was more than 250 feet above the water. To the south, they could see a boat ramp below them.

Hunter wondered how far the river went prior to merging with the Rio Grande. He knew it couldn't be far, because they had to be near the border. He was actually surprised he couldn't see the Rio Grande from where they stood.

Dr. Sanderson returned to the Suburban. Hunter was the only one who seemed to notice what he was doing. He watched him pull a driver club and a shopping bag out of the vehicle.

"Dr. Sanderson," he said, "where are you going with that club?"

"The driving range. You boys want to hit some balls?"

Dr. Sanderson followed a little trail down to another ledge. He took a golf ball out of the shopping bag and then tried his best to drive a tee into the rocky ground, to no avail. He ended up wedging the tee in between two rocks. After placing a ball on the tee, he took a practice swing with the beat-up driver. He then stepped closer to the tee, went into his backswing, and made solid contact with the little white ball.

The rest of the group watched the ball soar toward the Highway 90 bridge, which was easily more than a thousand yards to the north. From his angle, Hunter thought for a half a second that the ball might have the distance to reach the bridge, but then it dropped, far short, into the Pecos.

"I'll buy a beer for anyone who can outdrive me," shouted Dr. Sanderson. "Ty beat me for the first time last year."

Jack, the only serious golfer of the group, was the first one down the trail. He hit a major slice and yelled, "Fore!" The ball barely made it into the water.

One by one, the guys took their turn driving golf balls into the Pecos. Cole tried twice due to a complete miss on his first swing. No one even came close to Dr. Sanderson's first drive.

When the last member of the group had taken his shot, Dr. Sanderson made one more request. He set up a tripod with his Nikon pointed toward the rock wall and the Highway 90 bridge. While asking everyone to gather around for a group shot, he fiddled with the settings and timer on the camera. Once they were in place, he hit a button and rushed to join the group. He explained that he had many pictures of Ty and him in this same spot over the years and that the scene was too beautiful not to take a picture every time he was there.

As they pulled out from the scenic overlook and back onto Highway 90, Hunter looked into the rearview mirror at Cinco.

"You were right. I'm going to love it out here. This is awesome."

The sheer cliffs of the Pecos River crossing seemed to be the gateway to West Texas and the starting point of what promised to be an epic adventure. As they crossed over the bridge, Hunter felt like they were crossing over more than a river; it was almost as if they were crossing into a different time, a wild frontier that had somehow been shielded from the advances of modern-day society.

A few miles down the road, a sign for Langtry and the Judge Roy Bean Visitor Center were the only indications of civilization.

The museum, dedicated to the Old West–era judge who claimed to be "the Law West of the Pecos," made Hunter imagine what it was like out here when outlaws lived by the gun and Indians roamed the countryside. He tried to recall from his history studies whether the raiding Comanche bands made it this far south, into Mescalero-Apache territory. He didn't think so. From what he could remember, the western Hill Country was their southern boundary. But he did know that the fierce Comanche warriors pushed the militarily inferior Apaches south.

Beyond the signs for Langtry, which, from the highway, seemed to be no more than a few mobile homes and the museum, Dr. Sanderson pulled into a gas station that looked straight out of a scene from the movie *Giant*. Set in the 1940s and featuring James Dean and Rock Hudson, the film was a classic depiction of West Texas. Cole jumped out of the Suburban and entered the filling station's front door.

"Let's get some cold ones," Hunter said. He was curious to see the inside of the store.

When they entered, Cole explained, "Didn't want to run out of snuff between here and Sanderson."

There was no attendant, but they could see that someone was sitting in a recliner, watching an antiquated television set in a room on the other side of the register. Apparently, the station also served as living quarters. A middle-aged man, whose weathered skin and graying hair made him look older than he probably was, got out of his chair and greeted them. "Afternoon, boys."

Eyeing the beer fridge, Hunter asked Cole how far it was to Sanderson. The attendant matter-of-factly stated, "It's a six-pack."

"Well, sir, I think we'll have to test that theory," Hunter said.

"Sharp, grab a bag of ice." Chris was already reaching into the cooler for a case of Lone Star.

Hunter pulled a ten-pound bag of ice from a separate freezer and set it on the counter next to the case of beer.

"Where you boys headed?" the man said. It was clear that he hadn't had many visitors all day. Hunter explained that they were going to Big Bend—and why—as Chris paid for the beer and Cole's can of Copenhagen.

On the way out, both Chris and Hunter kept their composure until they got to the truck. Chris chuckled. "That was amazing. He actually told us to drink a six-pack between here and the next town."

Hunter nodded. "He wasn't fucking around. Said it with a straight face."

They worked together to fill the Yeti and the soft cooler they kept inside the truck. Hunter handed the cooler to Chris and said, "You have exactly six beers to drink before Sanderson, son."

Dr. Sanderson wasn't known for his patience, and he apparently didn't want to wait for them to get their beer situation under control. He was already back on the highway, doing eighty-five miles an hour by the time Hunter got back behind the steering wheel.

"The doctor isn't fucking around either." Chris motioned for him to get going. "Get on the road, man."

Hunter quickly buckled his seatbelt and threw the truck into gear as Chris gave Jack and Cinco a recap of their interaction with the gas station attendant.

"I told you," Cinco said. "It gets pretty western out here, boys."

Once they caught up to their lead vehicle, Hunter set the cruise control on eighty-five and sipped his cold Lone Star. It was apparent that Chris, Jack, and Cinco were intent on testing the Langtry filling station attendant's distance calculation.

The farther west they travelled, the rockier the terrain became, and the more the condition of Highway 90 deteriorated. The only vehicle they had seen since leaving Langtry was a green-and-white Border Patrol Tahoe towing a tractor tire on its side down the seemingly endless caliche road that ran parallel to the highway. The tire smoothed the road, allowing Border Patrol agents to see footprints if illegal aliens crossed it.

"You'd think with all of the technology today, they could find some better way to spend their time than to drag these roads," Cinco said.

Chris shook his head. "How would anybody survive out here on foot?"

"A lot of them don't," Hunter responded matter-of-factly.

About half an hour down the road, beyond a long draw that looked like it may have held water hundreds of years ago, the town of Dryden snuck up out of nowhere. A stucco wall, all that remained of an old building, was the first indication of civilization. A couple of pickup trucks, to Hunter's surprise, were parked out front of the only building in town that seemed to be inhabitable. The barely legible sign on the front of the building said something about groceries and meat, but Hunter couldn't make it all out as they passed. At the only intersection in town, a dirt road to the south led to a few other scattered buildings, and a dusty, paved ranch road to the north crossed over the railroad tracks running parallel to Highway 90 and disappeared into the horizon. As quickly as it had come, Dryden was gone in the rearview mirror.

"Holy shit!" Hunter slammed the breaks in response to Dr. Sanderson's Suburban suddenly slowing down from ninety miles an hour to somewhere around seventy. Fifteen minutes after passing through Dryden, the highway started to wind sharply around miniature mesas that were speckled with dots of green foliage. A black-and-white Texas Department of Public Safety State Trooper was parked on the side of the road around one of the turns.

"Thank God for radar detectors." Chris put his beer down in between his legs as they passed.

"Sanderson is right around one of these curves," Cinco pointed out, as if he were giving a tour.

Chris took a sip of his Lone Star and smirked. "We must be ahead of schedule; this is only number four."

Sanderson did appear around one of the curves, almost as if it had been carved out of the foothills on both sides. An old motel on the right revealed more activity than in Dryden, Langtry, and Comstock put together. The houses and businesses along the main street had brown rock front yards absent of any vegetation. Hunter dialed up Robert Earl Keen's "Rolling By," a ballad depicting a dusty West Texas town that Hunter imagined to be exactly like Sanderson. He quietly wondered if there was any relation between the town's namesake and Ty. This was certainly his kind of place.

Dr. Sanderson turned into the parking lot of the Prickly Pear liquor store. He and Cole got out of their vehicle and entered the rock dwelling.

"Time to stock up for the weekend," Chris said, already halfway out of the truck. The other three followed him into the store.

Dr. Sanderson had already picked out a couple of bottles of wine, and Cole had two cases of beer hooked under his arms. Cinco found his way to the Scotch section and secured a bottle of fifteen-year-old Glenlivet.

"This is for tonight and tomorrow after the hike, right?" Hunter inquired, not to anyone in particular but generally at the two from the other vehicle.

"Hot springs after the hike," Cole said. "Don't short yourself on the beer."

"Got it!" Hunter grabbed two cases of Lone Star Light from the refrigerator.

Chris took out two as well, put them on the counter, and then went back for a six-pack of tall-boy Coors Originals. Hunter looked at him inquisitively as Chris shrugged.

"Nothing wrong with a few yellow bellies for the road, man."

The six of them checked out of the store and gathered around the vehicles as they filled their respective coolers with beer and ice, stretched their legs, and generally shot the bull. There was a chill in the late afternoon air, but the sun, now in the west, was still up, and it felt good to be outside. It was noticeably less humid than where they had spent the previous night at the F bar R, and even less so compared with where they had started their journey in South Texas. Dr. Sanderson cut off the small talk without saying a word by firing up the Suburban.

"Do they play football out here?" Chris asked as they passed the bank and the couple of restaurants that made up downtown Sanderson, a town that had been nearly three times its current size of 837 in its heyday, when mohair and wool were produced there by the millions of pounds.

"Yes, sir," Cinco said. "Six-man is big time. Sharp, you would have dominated out here."

Hunter smiled at that comment. It was great to have friends remind him of the good ol' days.

Past the outskirts of town, a brown sign on the right side of the road read Big Bend National Park 132 Miles.

"Almost to Marathon, boys," Cinco announced.

The volume in the truck got considerably louder over the fifty-mile stretch between Sanderson and Marathon. Chris, Jack, and Cinco were well into their second six-pack apiece, and the louder their banter got, the louder Hunter turned up the stereo. As they approached the town of Marathon, the foothills began turning into mountain ranges in the distance. Cinco mentioned that the Glass Mountains were the closest to the north and that the Davis Mountains were a long way to the west.

Hunter, although he wasn't feeling anywhere close to as good as his travelling companions, already knew that he loved this vast beautiful country. There was something wild about this land, which greatly appealed to him. There was also a hint of loneliness settling in the farther they pushed west. It may have been the depressive effects of the hangover that had been looming all day, but it may have also been the element of desolation that came with this territory. Beautiful and desolate were not words that typically went well together, but Hunter couldn't think of two that better fit the description. One thing he was sure about was that there was a different breed of life west of the Pecos, and he wanted to experience it.

A couple of old gas stations were all of Marathon that Hunter and the rest of the group got to see prior to turning south on Highway 385, toward the national park. Cinco assured his traveling companions that they were in for a "big time" in Marathon the following night and that there was much more to see of the well-talked-about town.

They had to stop and wait for a slow-moving train passing through town on the tracks running across the highway. The train horn was clearly audible over the truck's stereo system as it rhythmically blasted the warning signals to anyone who may have ventured around the drop-arms guarding a crossing.

Hunter peered to the east in an attempt to find the end of the rusted freight cars, but the train went on as far as he could see. The whole scene seemed to be something out of the time where travel by rail was the norm and buffalo roamed the plains.

"Give me your camera, brother." Hunter looked back at Cinco and pointed at his bag. Cinco pulled out his digital camera and handed it forward.

"Y'all jump out for a picture." Hunter opened his door and stepped out onto the dusty highway. Cinco put on his felt hat, grabbed his beer, and followed Chris and Jack out of the truck on their side. Hunter directed them to stand on the east side of the road with the train coming from behind them. He set the camera to black and white and snapped a couple of shots of the three of them, all of them making the "horns up" symbol by holding their index and little fingers up to signify longhorn cattle horns, for the University of Texas.

Once the train passed, they were back on the road, headed south for the park. The sun had begun setting beyond the mountain ranges to the west, and the Chisos Mountains, the mountain range entirely within the national park, were becoming more and more visible to the south. This was the West Texas that Ty had raved about, yet the stories and pictures didn't quite do it the justice it deserved. It was so much more impressive in person.

Although the bullshit in the truck cab got louder with every beer,

Hunter was in his own world, sipping on a cold one, taking in the new country around him, and listening to the Townes Van Zandt tune "Dead Flowers." The song triggered thoughts of Ty. He knew Ty was close, somewhere off beyond those mountain peaks or possibly right there in the truck with them.

CHAPTER 8

RAVE

The sun had completely set by the time they drove through the empty guard shack at the entrance to the park. The sign said something about a park fee, but Dr. Sanderson didn't stop, so Hunter followed suit. Once inside the park, the two vehicles slowed to fifty-five miles an hour to somewhat obey the posted speed limit of forty-five. Twenty minutes later, they were passing a park headquarters at what the signs called Panther Junction. They kept moving, through pitch darkness, following the winding park highway to the Chisos Basin. Hunter slowed down after the first sharp turn, which, even in the dark, he could see was a sheer drop-off. He felt more comfortable with more distance between their truck and the Suburban.

"There's the lodge, boys." Cinco pointed to some lights down below when the road took a sharp turn to the right.

Hunter looked down at what appeared to be a headquarters building with several two-story motel buildings to the south. To his surprise, there appeared to be quite a few vehicles in the parking lots surrounding the motels. Once they were down the steep cliff, Dr. Sanderson pulled up in front of the headquarters building and came over to the truck. Hunter was already standing on the pavement when Dr. Sanderson relayed the plan.

"Let's check in," he said, "and then we'll head to Terlingua for dinner."

Hunter nodded. "Yes, sir. Sounds good."

All six of them went into the Chisos Mountain Lodge headquarters. Dr. Sanderson passed a young lady with multiple piercings who was working the front desk of the gift shop and headed to a desk farther in the store, where another female park employee sat. He and Cole checked in first, two men to a room, followed by Hunter and Cinco, and finally Chris and Jack. It was clear they weren't dealing with the park's sharpest employee, and the whole process seemed to take forever to Hunter, who was starting to get really hungry.

There appeared to be a lot of activity in the restaurant adjoining the gift shop, but Dr. Sanderson insisted that Terlingua was a better dinner option and worth the wait. When the lady manning the front desk heard that they were going to Terlingua, she made some comment about there being a rave there tonight. Hunter disregarded it, thinking there was no way that a restaurant Dr. Sanderson wanted to take them to would also be the type of place that would host a rave.

Once they were checked in, they got back into their vehicles and drove down the hill to the two-story lodge. Their three rooms were next to each other, each with twin beds and disappointingly similar to a low-end commercial motel room. Anxious to continue the exploration, Hunter threw his gear onto one of the beds, took a piss, and then left Cinco in the room. In the parking lot, he found Jack sitting on the tailgate of the truck, a bottle of high-end single malt Scotch and a sleeve of Styrofoam cups next to him.

"You need a roadie, bro?" Jack began pouring before Hunter had a chance to respond. A splash of water and ice filled the cup to the brim.

The beer buzz Hunter had developed on the drive was starting to fade, and he definitely needed a cocktail. "Gracias, señor." He graciously accepted the drink.

Jack continued to pour drinks as the rest of the group rallied in the parking lot.

Dr. Sanderson was the last one out. "Boys, let's head to Terlingua for some dinner."

It was clear he had no time for bullshit, and Hunter took his cue. "Yes, sir. We'll follow you." He and the other three quickly loaded into Cinco's pickup. Chris, who had called shotgun to reserve his previously held seat in the vehicle, also made sure that they had a full cooler of beer for the road trip of unknown duration.

Soon they were back on the winding road, heading out the way they came into the Chisos Basin, following the white Suburban in complete darkness. Hunter could barely make out the black outline of the mountain peaks that surrounded them. When they came to a familiar T at Highway 385, still in the park, the caravan turned to the west.

"Hunter, get some tunes going, my man." Jack was already at a higher level of drunkenness than the others and clearly wanted to liven up the rest of the group. Hunter hit shuffle, and "Southside of Heaven" by Ryan Bingham and the Dead Horses came on.

The band had become an overnight sensation on the Americana music scene in the last year, since the lead singer had cowritten and performed the theme song for the movie *Crazy Heart,* starring Jeff Bridges. Hunter cranked up the volume in response to pleas from the backseat.

"Mescalito, man!" Hunter said. "There's not a bad song on this album."

"Saw him in Houston a few months ago," Chris said. "He puts on a kick-ass show."

"Man, next time he comes close to SA or Houston, let's go see him." Hunter, who considered himself a Texas music connoisseur, had yet to see the band live. "He's all over the place now that he's a rock star."

Chris nodded. "Hope that rock star status doesn't change his music."

Hunter reflected on that comment in silence for several minutes. Everything good seemed to change, and he was quite confident Ryan Bingham would as well. Pat Green sure as hell had. The one-time dance-hall-playing Texas songwriter had turned Nashville-based country pop star. When Hunter was in high school, he was among the musician's original followers. Now he didn't even recognize Pat Green's latest work when it came on the radio.

After what seemed like endless miles of desert mountain terrain in pitch-black darkness, they turned off the highway onto Farm to Market Road 170, following the signs to Terlingua Ghost Town.

"Ghost town?" Jack said. "Where the fuck are we going, Sharp?"

"It's an old deserted mining town," Cinco answered. "Now it's just people looking to get completely off the grid livin' out here. I mean way off the grid, man."

"So it shouldn't be hard to score some peyote with the locals?" Chris was looking back at Cinco from his front seat with a smile. Laughter erupted from all four of the truck's passengers.

"James, you would fit right in with these fuckin' hippies," Jack commented and finished off what was left of his beer.

"Better here than with you cocksuckers in Dallas," Chris fired back.

Hunter grinned at that comment and quietly agreed, knowing that Ty would have felt the same way. He couldn't think of a worse punishment than living in Dallas. There was no doubt in his mind that, if given the choice, living out here with only generator power and no connection to the modern-day world would beat the hell out of living in Dallas. He wasn't sure whether it was the city, the people, or both that turned him off so much, but as far as he was concerned, it might as well be on another planet from the rest of Texas.

A few miles down the road, he noticed the signs and cars parked out in front of a dimly lit bar. "That's La Kiva," Cinco said. "We need to stop there for a drink on the way back."

Hunter nodded. "If you say so, man. I mean this crew isn't hard to please."

Cinco smirked and took a slow sip of his cold beer. "I've heard it's worth the stop."

The crew was clearly getting restless as they pushed on for several miles through the Terlingua darkness, an indication to Hunter that they were out of beers in the backseat.

"Man I hope we're almost there," he said. "I'm fuckin' parched."

As soon as the words left his mouth, the Suburban put on its right-turn signal and slowly veered up a poorly paved road. They drove up to a row of buildings that looked like they belonged on

Main Street in an Old West frontier town. Two storefronts in a single building were connected to the stucco Starlight Theatre by a boardwalk lined with rock. The Starlight looked to be a happening place; there were at least eight or nine cars parked in the gravel lot.

Everyone was out of the truck before Hunter had killed the engine.

"Heading for the outhouse, boys," Jack said and made a beeline for an actual outhouse at the end of the boardwalk.

They waited for Dr. Sanderson and Cole and then walked up to the restaurant bar.

A small group of people loitered outside the front door, smoking cigarettes. They weren't dressed in what Hunter would consider typical West Texas garb. Two of the three were scantily clothed women, and the third was a man, about Hunter's age, with a full scraggly beard, shoulder-length hair, and more piercings than Hunter had ever seen on one human being. To top it off, he was wearing huge round sunglasses, although it had been dark for hours.

"Y'all here for the rave?" one of the women asked.

"Naw," Cole replied. "Just dinner." His confused tone made his answer almost sound like a question.

Beyond the door of the 1930s-era mining-town theater, there was more of the same. The restaurant bar, lit up with strings of Christmas lights, was relatively full, and everyone inside looked more like the group out front than their group of six in boots and jeans. A scene from the movie *Animal House* popped into Hunter's mind: The music stops, and the crowd inside the bar—who are all black—turn to stare at the very white main characters and their dates walking in the front door. He removed his felt hat and looked around for a free table.

Someone by the bar said, "Who are these vaqueros?" which added to his level of discomfort.

Laughing, Dr. Sanderson walked up to the bar and ordered a beer. His move somewhat broke the ice for their group of friends, who spread out around the bar to try to order drinks. Chris got to the bartender first, ordered a round of margaritas for the group, and asked, "What's happening here tonight?"

"It's our annual rave!" answered the bartender. Somewhat cute, she had medium-length dark hair and was clearly braless in a white halter top. When she talked, Hunter could see a small, neon-green glow stick that she was playing with in her mouth.

A table became available shortly after drinks were served. They sat down, still gawking at the strange, out-of-place outfits, piercings, and behaviors. In the back of the restaurant was a stage, where the man from outside was setting up his DJ equipment. Hunter took a big swig of margarita and laughed as he surveyed the room.

"I mean, not exactly what I pictured out here," he said to no one in particular.

Jack walked over from the bar, margarita in hand, with the bartender. She passed out menus as he made the formal introduction.

"This is Chrissy. She goes to Sul Ross, and she assured me those are real." He pointed at her large breasts, which were hard to miss through her shirt.

"Nice," Cinco said. "Very classy."

"Gentlemen," she spoke primarily to Dr. Sanderson, "you picked a great night to join us at the Starlight. Our special is the chicken-fried steak. You may want to get your orders in pretty quick, though, because our chef is planning to shut down and join the rave in about twenty minutes."

Hunter noticed that although they all laughed at her instructions, she was being completely serious.

"As long as he hasn't already joined the rave." Cole had a sincere look of concern on his face.

The group was ready for another round of drinks by the time Chrissy had returned to take their orders. Everyone nodded to Hunter's "¿Uno más margarita?" call except Dr. Sanderson, who ordered a beer.

"Boys, I'm gonna tell you," he said, "that mountain is no walk in the park. Take it easy tonight."

Cole said something about Dr. Sanderson getting soft in his old age, and the next round of margaritas was on its way with their food orders.

Nearly an hour and a third round of margaritas later, their food came out. By this time, they were the only ones who were still eating. The chef, as Chrissy had accurately predicted, had come out with their food and announced that the kitchen was closed. He then took a shot of something handed to him from someone standing at the bar.

Hunter looked around the table at his group of hungry and now adequately buzzed friends and felt good about where he was at this particular moment. He met eyes with Dr. Sanderson, who nodded, as if he had read Hunter's mind, and then turned back to his conversation with Cole.

"You doing alright, bud?" Cinco asked.

"Yes, sir. It's just good to be here, you know?"

Cinco nodded as he sipped his margarita. "I know, man. This is going to be a great trip."

Hunter nearly inhaled his chicken-fried steak while downing his fourth margarita. As he reached his last bite, Chrissy was back with yet another round. Dr. Sanderson was the only one, despite further harassment from several at the table, who declined in favor of iced tea. Hunter gave his warning about the hike half a second of thought, but he was having too good a time to even consider slowing down. All of his closest friends had somehow made it to Terlingua, Texas, to celebrate the life of one of their own. The reality was Hunter didn't know how to celebrate that sober. Generally speaking, he found being in social settings, even with some of the people closest to him, difficult while sober. Part of it was the fear of coming down; part of it was insecurity and anxiety. That, compiled with the emotion surrounding Ty's death, had the potential to turn Hunter into a figurative train wreck—at least it'll be a fun train wreck—with no thought of taking his foot off of the gas.

The guy who had greeted them at the front door was now on the old theater's stage behind a DJ booth, still wearing his big round sunglasses and starting to turn some of his records. A mix of electronic-sounding dance music filled the small confines of the theater. The locals moved toward the dance floor with their glow sticks and Hula-Hoops in hand. Photos of Big Bend National Park started scrolling on a screen that had been hung from the ceiling behind the stage.

"Things are fixin' to get weird in here," Cole said.

"I don't think we quite know what weird is yet," Cinco added.

"You boys never been to a rave before?" Chris was laughing.

Before long, the dance floor was packed—as much as it could be with everyone having a Hula-Hoop swinging around their hips.

Chrissy came over to let them know that she would be behind the bar or on the dance floor if they needed anything. Collectively, the group decided to order a round of beers.

"You sure, man?" Chris said to Hunter. "If we have another round of 'ritas, I might get you out there in one of those Hula-Hoops."

Hunter laughed at the thought. No matter how drunk he was, he didn't think anyone could get him to Hula-Hoop to techno music.

Jack was the last to order his beer. He winked at Chrissy and slyly commented, "I'll see you out on the dance floor, darlin'." Equally slyly, she slowly removed the glow stick from her mouth and smiled at him before turning back to the bar for the round of beers.

As promised, Jack was out on the dance floor fifteen minutes later, glow stick in one hand, beer in the other. A Hula-Hoop awkwardly rotated once or twice around him and Chrissy before falling to the floor. She was laughing hysterically at his antics, which Hunter found to be slightly irritating.

They were all standing now, beers in hand, at the edge of the dance floor, taking the rave in one sip at a time. It looked like a scene from a junior high dance, with the girls out on the dance floor and a line of boys staring awkwardly from afar. In this case, it was not a division of boys and girls as much as it was cultures—cowboys and hippies—although Hunter wasn't sure you could call these people hippies. It was the bizarre blend of hippie and techno dance music that he was having trouble reconciling. One thing he was sure about was that there was more than alcohol driving the dance moves on display in the Starlight.

One more round of beers was enough to convince Hunter and most of the group that it was time for a change of scenery. He was convinced that the locals were as anxious for them to leave as he was, and he reminded Cinco of his earlier suggestion to have a nightcap at La Kiva, the bar they had seen coming into Terlingua. Cinco nodded back at him and made a circular motion in the air with his index finger as if to say, Round 'em up!

Jack was the only one who protested the decision to move on. "Come on, Sharp," he said. "Things are just starting to get interesting."

Hunter nodded with half a smirk on his face. "Nelson, you're welcome to stay. Good luck getting back to the park. Can you close me out, Chrissy?"

Hunter was the first back to Cinco's truck. He listened to more Ryan Bingham tunes as he waited for his buddies. Jack was the last out, swaying and almost falling off of the wood-plank boardwalk. When he finally got in the truck, he was met with a barrage of insults.

Cinco was the hardest on him. "Don't forget your glow stick, you fuckin' douche bag."

Jack clearly wasn't sober enough to respond quickly, so he gave the entire truck the middle finger.

"Nelson, did you get her digits, man?" Chris inquired.

Jack held up his iPhone so everyone could see his latest entry: "Chrissy" and a phone number. Again, he silently extended his middle finger to the other three. The gesture was met with roaring laughter.

Somewhere between Terlingua Ghost Town and La Kiva, Hunter started laughing. "You know shit was fixin' to get real weird in there once we left."

Chris laughed. "They probably barred the door once we were out of there."

"Don't worry, boys," Cinco said. "There won't be any raves at La Kiva."

The number of cars in the La Kiva parking lot had dwindled down to three or four, and to Hunter, it seemed even darker than when they passed it the first time. The dimly lit storefront looked like the entrance to a mine shaft: A wood-beam frame held the bar's sign, and a wooden doorway, with not much of a building structure behind it, slanted down into the ground. Cinco was the first one through the door and down the steps into the bar. Hunter followed suit and was surprisingly impressed with what he discovered through the swinging doors at the bottom of the stairwell.

Rock walls surrounded a small wooden bar. There were a lot of redwood tables, and the ceiling was made of beautiful wood rafters. Hunter affirmed Cinco's earlier recommendation by saying, "This place is cool, man."

"Wait 'til you see the back porch," Cinco said.

The bartender at La Kiva was, in Hunter's estimation, nowhere near as good-looking as Chrissy. He stood about six foot three, probably weighed over 250 pounds, had hair down past his shoulders and a Grizzly Adams–style full beard. He had a relatively unfriendly disposition about him, and his black long-sleeve T-shirt read Guns don't kill people; I kill people. He fit perfectly in the dimly lit dungeon.

Cinco ordered two Coors Lights. The bartender nodded and reached for his refrigerator. They paid for their beers, and Hunter followed Cinco out the back door to the porch, commenting, "That guy is going to love Nelson."

They were the only ones in the back porch area, which was darker than inside the bar. There were a few picnic tables, a stage, and a bricked-in barbeque pit that was still smoking from the evening's menu.

"Before we sit down, we've got to see the dungeon." Cinco pointed to another rock opening.

"They have another dungeon besides the bar?" Hunter was a little bit creeped out. They took the stairs down into the "dungeon," aided by the light from their cellphones. Hunter thought it looked like it could have been a nuclear bomb shelter from the 1960s. The elongated rock-and-concrete room was completely empty.

"There's really not much to see," Cinco said. He was already headed back up the stairs by the time Hunter got to the bottom of the staircase. "It's weird enough that you've got to at least come down here."

Hunter took one final look around. "What the fuck do they use this for?"

"Who knows, man?" Cinco was already back at the top of the stairs and out of the rock enclosure.

The rest of the group eventually made their way out to the back porch area, took the tour of the dungeon, and then sat down at the picnic tables.

"You've got to see the pisser," Cole said. "It's a cast-iron pot hangin' from the wall with some kind of potpourri in it." Hunter got a kick out of hearing the ranch hand say potpourri and pisser in the same sentence.

"Only in Terlingua, boys." Dr. Sanderson smiled and shook his head.

Two more rounds of drinks came and went quickly. Dr. Sanderson, who had stuck to iced tea, suggested that the group take the party back to the park. "Park rangers may be out on the roads, and we don't need any of you boys going to jail tonight," he said. The voice of reason had spoken.

No one had any objections to leaving La Kiva; they had seen what they had come to see, and there was plenty of cold beer back at the lodge. Cinco pointed at Jack, who was telling stories that didn't make any sense at a totally inappropriate volume considering the stone silence otherwise, and issued a challenge.

"Nelson, you ready to lose some money on the washer pit?"

Washers had always been a favorite beer-drinking pastime for Hunter and his friends, and any worthwhile beer-drinking pastime had to be gambled on. Jack had a bad habit of getting drunk and losing money. All indications were that it could be a rough weekend for the senator's son. Although everyone else had ordered beers, Jack had switched to whiskey. He looked barely conscious.

He flashed a closed-mouth grin back at Cinco, his eyes slightly open. "Bring it, amigo. I'm just hitting my prime."

Hunter knew there was no way he should be driving, but he estimated he was in as good a shape as anyone else in the truck. Dr. Sanderson volunteered to take the lead, so all Hunter had to do was follow his brake lights and keep the truck between the lines, of which he had become a self-proclaimed expert. Cinco took shotgun and managed the music at Hunter's request.

"I got ya, brother. You concentrate on staying on the road." Cinco turned up the volume to Guy Clark's "Out in the Parking Lot," yet another tune inspired by the region.

Chris poked his head in between them from the middle backseat. "Sharp has never let us down," he said. "Don't doubt the man."

Chris's comment brought back a flood of memories from college for Hunter. He had always been the driver, and truth be told, he enjoyed it. There was something about driving with a good buzz, tunes playing on the radio, particularly out on country ranch roads at night, that was dangerously appealing to him. He knew it would catch up to him at some point, as it had with so many of his friends, but there was still that wild streak in him that he had trouble controlling after a certain threshold of alcohol intake. His and Cinco's exploits in Mexico the night before were evidence enough that he still had a propensity to make bad decisions. The good news was that, in his mind, there was a point of drunkenness where he felt that he would be too drunk to drive and at which point he knew he wouldn't put himself or anyone else at risk. In college, there had been no such point and very little fear of getting caught, which contributed to a recklessness that scared him a little now to think about.

The two-vehicle caravan pulled back into the lodge parking lot right after midnight. Dr. Sanderson and Cole bid the rest of the group good night and imparted one last warning about the severity of the hike in the morning. Hunter opened up the doors to the Chevy pickup and turned the music on loud enough that it was audible in the parking lot but wouldn't disturb anyone trying to sleep in their rooms. The mood was a little more low-key, which was aided by several slow-paced Willie Nelson and Townes Van Zandt songs played one after another.

Cinco had built a makeshift washer pit out of two-foot square wood boxes with a two-inch hole in the middle of each one. He carried the two pits around with him in the bed of his truck, apparently for occasions like this one. He spaced the boxes approximately twenty-one feet from each other in the parking lot. The objective of the game was to pitch the inch-in-diameter washers, closest to the hole. Cinco might as well have held a major in throwing washers, as much as he played the game growing up and through college.

Unfortunately for him, Cinco wouldn't get to follow through on his challenge to Jack, who passed out on the way back from La Kiva and was sound asleep in the cab of the truck. Cinco made himself a tall Scotch on the rocks in a Styrofoam cup and looked at Hunter. "You game, brother?"

Hunter nodded. "Five bucks a game?" No game could be played in this group without some kind of wager, but Hunter felt like starting slow, particularly while facing the semiprofessional washer-throwing skills of Cinco White.

Sometime between games, Cinco convinced Chris and Hunter to mix Scotch drinks. He had already finished his first and was damn near going to fight anyone who refused to have another one with him. Chris, being in the best shape of the three and not involved in the now-heated washers match, lined up the cups on Cinco's tailgate, filled them with ice from the Yeti cooler, and poured one last round of drinks. By the time he handed them out, Hunter had put himself into a forty-dollar hole.

"Damn it! Double-or-nothing!" he pleaded with Cinco as his opponent's washer found the hole to beat him once again.

"You're as bad as Nelson," commented Chris as he handed over the cocktail.

Hunter knew they were both on the downhill slope of the drinking-game bell curve, his skill peaking with a good buzz and then falling off sharply with a few more drinks, but he was bound and determined to win his money back.

Cinco nodded. "Gotta admire your spirit, brother. Eighty it is."

Hunter took a big initial sip of the whiskey, leaned forward with a washer in his right hand, and tried desperately to focus on the hole in the board next to Cinco.

The match ended up in a narrow defeat once again, and Hunter decided it was time to cut his losses rather than play the $160 double-or-nothing game Cinco offered. It was after three in the morning, the Scotch had hurt more than the washer's loss, and it was time to either throw up or go to bed.

"Who's going to take Nelson to bed?" Cinco asked.

Hunter looked at Chris. "He's your roommate," he said. "You want to fuck with it?"

Chris didn't hesitate. "Shit no. He can sleep in the truck."

Hunter looked back at Cinco and said, "There's your answer."

CHAPTER 9

THE MOUNTAIN

Eight thirty came quickly that morning. Hunter woke up to Cole's voice and a banging on the door of their room.

"Leavin' in thirty minutes, boys," shouted a voice through the door. "Better get breakfast if you're gonna do it."

In the other twin bed, Cinco didn't even budge. Hunter tried to lift his still fully clothed body off of the top of the covers, but the pounding ache in his head seemed to take control and prevent any movement.

"Cinco, get up brother. We gotta get goin'."

Cinco, also still in his jeans and boots, rolled over and asked, "What the fuck happened last night?"

Finding that question somewhat amusing, Hunter replied: "Rave."

"I gotta stop hanging out with you, Sharp," Cinco said, as if Hunter had in any way been responsible for all of the tequila and Scotch he'd pounded. "You think Nelson was confused when he woke up in my truck this morning?" That thought made them both laugh.

Ten minutes went by before Hunter could make himself get into the shower. Despite the headache, he was pretty sure he was still completely drunk and being on his feet confirmed that for him. Somehow, he managed to pull on his lightweight fishing pants, a long-sleeve T-shirt, and his New Balance running shoes. Cinco, who had foregone the shower for a few extra minutes in bed, had run out to his truck to grab a few bottles of water and left the door wide open, letting in the bright and painful sunlight. Hunter donned his Costa Del Mar sunglasses and sat down on the bed to tie his shoes.

"Everybody's waitin' on us, amigo." Cinco tossed him a bottle of water.

"I'm ready. Did they eat breakfast?"

Cinco nodded. "The smart ones did. Cole and Ty's dad have been up for over an hour. I've got some venison summer sausage we can eat on the trail."

Hunter put his head in his hands and answered sarcastically, "That sounds amazing."

Cinco finished getting dressed, put on brand-new hiking boots, donned a baseball cap, filled up his Camelbak hydration pack, and was back out the door with a spring in his step that Hunter found slightly irritating.

Hunter was the last one out to the parking lot, where the gathered group looked like something out of an REI commercial. He was the only one who wasn't wearing some kind of hiking boots, and everyone else had Camelbaks. Ty's dad had a telescopic walking stick that looked like a ski pole. The only other person who stood out was Cole, who looked like the ranch hand that he was, wearing tight Wrangler jeans and a tucked-in, starched button-down shirt. Although Jack looked as bad as Hunter felt, he was decked out in brand-name hiking clothing and gear that looked like he had pulled off the price tags this morning.

"Did I miss the memo on the hiking gear?" Hunter inquired with a sarcastic tone.

"I've got to at least look like I know what I'm doing," Jack replied in an extremely groggy voice.

"You're goin' to wish you had some gear in about an hour." Dr. Sanderson sounded like one of his old football coaches with this counsel. Hunter chose to respectfully ignore the commentary and downed the entire bottle of water Cinco had delivered to him. He tried to hide his shaking hands from Dr. Sanderson, but he was quite sure it was obvious to everyone.

The trail to San Isabel Peak began a few hundred yards from the park headquarters. It was enough distance to warrant driving from the lodge rather than walking up the main park road. There was a ten-space parking lot on the side of the road with no clear signage as to what it was for or any indication that it was the starting point of a trail.

Sitting in the passenger's seat of Cinco's truck, Hunter studied the map of the park that Chris had picked up in the headquarters earlier that morning. "The trail to San Isabel isn't marked on this map," he said, still searching.

"That's because there isn't a trail," Chris said. "I asked the dude at the information desk the same question. I told him we were going to San Isabel, and all he said was 'Good luck.' I don't think Ty's dad was fuckin' around when he said this was going to be a hike."

The group unloaded, ensured they had everything they needed

in their packs, and continued attempting to hydrate after the previous night's activities. Dr. Sanderson insisted on a prehike group picture, telling Hunter that he wanted to make sure he got a picture with everyone, in case not everyone—namely, Hunter—made it back alive. As a friendly passerby took their picture in the middle of the road, Hunter started to become anxious about how bad he was starting to feel and about how difficult this hike might turn out to be. Failing to make it up the mountain because of heavy drinking the night before would be inexcusable in the eyes of Dr. Sanderson, especially after all the warnings he had given. Hunter was already sweating profusely, which was in no way related to the temperate sixty-five-degree weather, and his legs were almost as shaky as his trembling hands.

"You all right, brother?" Cinco asked.

Even though the picture had been taken, Hunter had not moved from his spot. He was wondering how many times Cinco had asked him that question. "Yeah, man. Just tryin' to get up for this."

The first couple hundred yards or so was a wide dirt trail with a very slight incline. Dr. Sanderson took the lead and looked back at Hunter and Cinco. "Keep up with me boys," he said. "Don't let an old man beat you. Ty would be the first one up the mountain."

The last part resonated with Hunter, and, regardless of how hungover—or drunk—he was, he was determined to keep up with the leader.

Hunter had another motivation in the back of his mind as well: He was convinced that Dr. Sanderson already thought poorly of him for what had happened with Stacy and didn't want him to think he was weak on top of it. If he was going to drink heavily and stay up all night, he had to show that he was tough enough to hang the next day. Even more concerning was Dr. Sanderson's realization that he was still completely drunk. Nevertheless, he was going to make it through this hike.

He felt every grade increase as the trail narrowed and steepened rapidly. His legs felt heavy and tight, but not nearly to the degree of tightness he felt in his chest. He was almost gasping for air.

"Man, I'm out of shape," he said to no one in particular.

It was all he could get out between breaths. He thought for a second that his shortness of breath may have had to do with the elevation but then admitted to himself that it was more likely something to do with the three-day binge.

They reached a rock formation, where the trail ended at an incredible vantage point, turning back in toward the mountain.

"That's where we're going, boys," Dr. Sanderson said, pointing upward and to the south, at a square sheer rock cliff, seemingly several thousand feet above them. From the road, it had looked impossible to climb without rock-climbing gear, but from this vantage point, Hunter could see a narrow path they'd have to climb to get behind the summit. Either way, it looked treacherous, and there was still a hell of a long way to go. They each took the opportunity to climb up on the rock formation, which was only big enough for one at a time, and take a look before turning around and continuing up the mountain.

After what seemed like at least another mile upward on the winding mountainside path, the incline leveled off, and the thick piñon tree cover broke over an open hilltop. The grassy peak revealed a spectacular view of the park from the other side of the mountain. Dr. Sanderson removed his pack and sat down in the grass, gazing out at the view.

Hunter sucked down an entire bottle of water. He chose not to remove his backpack prior to sitting down; his shirt was soaked through with sweat, and the breeze on the unprotected peak brought on a chill, and the pack kept his back covered and warm. He was pretty sure he was starting to sober, but the hangover was starting to creep in with increasing shakiness and a general feeling of malaise.

Cinco sat down next to him and, between sucks from the tube coming out of his backpack, asked Dr. Sanderson, "Are we halfway there?"

Without adjusting his gaze from the breathtaking view, Dr. Sanderson calmly replied, "We're about a quarter of the way."

After he'd snapped a couple of pictures, Dr. Sanderson was up and leading the way again. The other five slowly rose from their seated or kneeling positions, readjusted their packs, and followed him up a new and steeper incline. As they got a little higher, Hunter was surprised to see snow in spots that were shaded from the sun. Chris, who seemed to be faring better than the rest of the group, apparently couldn't resist the temptation to make a miniature snowball with the mud-stained snow. He threw it right at Hunter, who was too tired to make any attempt at dodging it. Instead, he waved his hand lazily at the oncoming projectile, resulting in his green-mirrored sunglasses getting splattered with snow and mud.

"Come on, Sharp!" Chris taunted. "Be an athlete,"

Hunter tried to catch his breath to respond but could only muster, "Fuck off, man."

After another hour of walking with several short breaks, the trail, now not much wider than what a whitetail deer would make on its path to a feeder, came to an abrupt end at the foot of a tremendous incline. Hunter estimated it was at a seventy-five to eighty-degree angle. The entire slope was covered with loose shale rock. Dr. Sanderson got down on all fours and began clawing his way up the loose rocks, creating miniature landslides in his wake. Chris and Cole were close behind him, looking more like mountain goats than hikers as they seemed to effortlessly zigzag their way up the incline.

Hunter's heart felt like it was going to beat out of his chest, and his lungs screamed for air, even before he started up the daunting mountainside. He was definitely no longer drunk, but the throbbing headache and uncontrollable shaking indicated that the effects of the booze were nowhere near leaving his system. The New Balances didn't help, providing zero support to his ankles as he took the first step onto the shale rock.

On top of a serious hangover, his OCD was cranking at full speed. Repetitive, nonsensical—but disturbing, nonetheless—negative thoughts seemed to be yet another mountain he was climbing internally. He doubted everything he rationally knew to be true about himself, about others, and about the world around him. The what ifs created a paralyzing fear that was only compounded by his efforts to answer them. His head was telling him to quit and focus on the distressing thoughts, but his heart kept his legs moving.

This internal conflict was all too familiar to him from years past, during football workouts and grueling fourth quarters, where he was forced to battle both physical and mental fatigue with a brain that seemed only to sabotage him. While there were times when the chronic condition got the best of him, the fact that he had been successful at all reflected tremendous mental toughness in the face of extreme levels of anxiety and fear.

This mountain was no place to lose focus. About halfway up

the incline and completely lost in thought, he put his weight forward prematurely on what he thought was a stable rock. Everything below him gave way, and he lost his footing. His knees hit first, and he felt a sharp stone cut right through his pants to scrape his right kneecap. He instinctively reached for something to grab onto, to slow his downward slide, and immediately regretted it as his right hand found a cactus.

"Son of a bitch!" He was pretty sure they could hear him yelling back in Marathon, sixty miles away.

"You alright, bud?" Cinco was now several feet above where Hunter's slide had started. He began descending to give Hunter a hand.

"I'm good, man," Hunter said. "Keep moving." He didn't want any help getting back up, and his pride was wounded more than his knee or hand.

He wouldn't be the last one up the rocks, which gave him some consolation. As he struggled to find his grip on something stationary, he looked back to see Jack, bent over, hands on his knees, a clear liquid spewing from his mouth.

"Don't get any on that nice North Face, pretty boy," Chris shouted from about twenty yards uphill.

Without replying, Jack straightened up and began to climb.

Hunter gave a half-second's thought to questioning why he chose to live the lifestyle that he had and to wondering about the toll that it must be taking on his body, realizing that it wasn't a choice as much as something in his genes, a hell-raising character defect that had been passed down generation to generation. He pushed on up the loose shale.

"We're almost there, boys!" Dr. Sanderson had navigated the

shale with relative ease and was leaning his pack against a rock as big as a full-ton pickup truck. Once the rest of the group was level with Dr. Sanderson, they could see that there was one more valley between them and their destination, although, from this angle, their destination peak didn't look nearly as daunting as it had from the other side with its sheer drop-off.

The valley, fully lit in the midday sun, was covered with brown grass that came up to their knees. Hunter appreciated the downhill jaunt, which allowed him to catch both his breath and the leader of the group. Dr. Sanderson was nearly in a sprint at this point, but the other five were right at his heels. When they hit the bottom of the valley and started up the mild incline on the other side, no one stopped for a break. Hunter could hear the words of his old football coaches—"Finish strong"—as he willed himself to make it up the final rise.

What rewarded them at the top far exceeded any of Hunter's expectations. The rock formation that made up San Isabel Peak was square and no wider than twenty yards across at any point. It was the highest peak as far as the eye could see, and the clarity on this January day had Hunter convinced he could see all the way to the Pacific Ocean. A brisk north wind cut right through his sweat-soaked clothing and sent a chill down his spine, yet it wasn't the cold that had all of the hair on his skin standing straight up. This was it—the place Ty had always described as heaven. The vast beauty of West Texas and northern Mexico lay below them. There wasn't any way God's view could be any more spectacular.

"Pretty special, bud." Cinco put his arm around Hunter's neck and was staring off into the distance to the south.

"It's unbelievable," Hunter said, finally catching his breath. He managed to smile. Words could not describe the figurative high he felt as he returned Cinco's embrace and took in the scenery. His hangover was gone, apparently sweated out somewhere along the brutal hike, and jubilation had taken its place. A tremendous sense of accomplishment had set in, replacing the self-doubt and urge to quit. High fives and hugs went all around. Even Jack, who was the last one to the top, was greeted by Chris with a firm handshake and a congratulatory smile.

"Welcome to San Isabel Peak, gentleman." Dr. Sanderson reached into his pack and pulled out a bottle of red wine. He made quick work of opening it with a custom-monogramed corkscrew. "I've been saving this bottle for a special occasion, and being here with you guys is as special as it gets." He handed each of them a small plastic cup and then poured each about half full. The six of them formed a loose circle, one foot toward the middle, wine in one hand, and the other hand on someone else's shoulder.

"Here's to Ty Bauman Sanderson for bringing all of us together on this mountain and to all of you for making this trip with me," Dr. Sanderson said, raising his glass. "This was his favorite place on earth, and he's smiling down on us today. God bless y'all." He lifted his cup and took a sip of his wine.

Dr. Sanderson's toast was met with smiles all around, and Hunter suddenly felt a sense of camaraderie with the group that rivaled that of a fraternity pledging. This group of men, bonded together by the loss of a beloved friend and son, had embarked on what would surely become an annual pilgrimage.

The next thirty minutes were spent taking pictures and enjoying the scenery that, of the group, only Dr. Sanderson had known to exist. Even Cinco, who had been to the park, commented on not having any idea there was a peak of this magnitude and beauty in this part of the world. The fact that it was off of any mapped trail and discovered only by those adventurous enough to get to it had ensured that it was a well-kept secret.

The wine was polished off, a can of Copenhagen was passed around, and the constant banter that had not stopped since the beginning of the hike slowly came to a silent halt. A combination of the breathtaking scenery and a reflection on the real purpose of their excursion seemed to come over the group.

Dr. Sanderson was the first to break the silence. "Did y'all bring your homework?" He'd sent an email before the trip, requesting that they each bring something that reminded them of their friendship with Ty. Each object would be placed with the ashes and buried in this final resting place.

Hunter chose to speak for the group. "Yes, sir. I think we all have something." He reached into his pack and pulled out a Steve Earle CD, *Train a Comin'*. The album featured Ty's favorite song, "Ben McCulloch." The ballad was written from the perspective of a Civil War–era Confederate infantryman, and Ty had loved everything about it. Hunter loved it because it embodied Ty, a natural-born soldier but also a rebel at heart. Inside the CD jacket, he'd included a picture of the two of them in their Alamo Heights football uniforms their senior year in high school. Ty had played defensive end. He was never the biggest or fastest player but was damn sure the toughest Hunter had ever played with.

Dr. Sanderson took a foldout spade from his pack and chose a shaded spot next to a mature tree to start digging. He shoveled away some fairly big rocks and then made quick work of what small amount of dirt he could move out of the hole. He removed the cedar chest from his pack and set it on the ground next to the freshly dug hole. He then removed the red bandana he had tied around his neck, kissed it, and placed it at the bottom of the hole.

"He wore this bandana the last time we were here," he said.

He opened the chest, and with his bare hands, he shoveled some ashes, probably about half of what had been inside, and dropped them delicately on top of the bandana.

Hunter moved to Dr. Sanderson's side, holding the CD. "He was every bit as tough as this song," he said, "and he would make me play it over and over again on the way to the ranch." He laughed, but amid the tears, it sounded more like a cough. He gently placed the CD over the ashes in the hole and stepped back to let Cinco get close.

Cinco had a picture of Ty, Hunter, and himself from their sophomore year in high school. Ty had been the first of their friends to turn sixteen, and the three of them were posing in front of the beat-up three-quarter-ton Ford pickup Dr. Sanderson had bought him. That seemed like ages ago to Hunter, and he couldn't believe how young they all looked. He hadn't filled out into his tall frame yet, and he looked as awkward and skinny as a beanpole. He remembered the excitement of finally having a buddy who could drive them around and the craziness of that ensuing summer.

"We thought we were pretty cool back then," Cinco said. "Ty kept talking about all of the chicks we would be picking up in his new truck, but it was usually just the three of us." Cinco placed the photograph in the hole and held his hand in place on top of the ashes.

"We miss you a lot, bud."

He pulled out an unopened can of Copenhagen from his

Camelbak. "I'm pretty sure that, in high school and his couple of years of college, he never had his own can. I think he dipped more of my snuff than I did." The line was met with laughter all around.

"He always made it worth my while with his bullshit." Cinco placed the can in the hole. "I'll look forward to the next time, amigo."

Cole held up an enormous six-point whitetail shed horn. "This was going to be his deer this year. We had seen him on camera over the last couple of years, and Ty kept sayin' this was the year, but he vanished on us. It's just as well. No one hunted that deer harder than Ty, and it wouldn't be right for someone else to shoot him. Rest in peace, Ty, nobody else is gonna kill your deer." He laid the shed horn next to the hole.

Chris unfolded a piece of paper that he had pulled out of the breast pocket on his shirt. "I'm still working on the last verse, and I didn't bring a copy to leave here, but I might as well read it to you now. I wrote a song about Ty." Chris was the musically talented guitar player of their group of college friends, and he had written several of his own songs, including some that more well-known artists had covered. He read the lyrics aloud:

> "Wild as West Texas, he lived hard and fast,
> Blew through our lives so quickly, no time to worry about the past.
> A son, a dad, a brother, a husband, and a friend,
> His time came too soon, but he was strong 'til the end.
>
> "He went off and joined the army, never lost a fight,
> Until he got that diagnosis, and left us that December night.
> Tough as nails, no one more genuine,

His time came too soon, but he was strong 'til the end.

"Climbing this West Texas mountain,
Make the pilgrimage, closest thing on earth to heaven.
We all loved him, blessed to call him a friend.
His time came too soon, but he was strong 'til the end."

By the time Chris finished reading the lyrics, Hunter had noticed that Dr. Sanderson had tears streaming down his cheeks. He put his right arm awkwardly around the grieving father's shoulder and half hugged him in an effort to provide some consolation. No one spoke, but everybody made eye contact with Chris, giving him nods of encouragement. In the silence, Chris folded up the lyrics and tucked them back into his breast pocket.

Jack gave the last tribute. An avid golfer, he had actually saved a scorecard from their freshman year at Texas. "I saved this because I thought it might have been the highest score I'll ever see and to give Ty shit about it when I saw him. He told me he was a good golfer. He showed up drunk from the night before, pounded Bloody Marys, and ended up fifty-three strokes over par. He parred eighteen to save the one-twenty-five. I'll give him credit that he didn't cheat and refused to quit a hole early. The round took over six hours, and the marshal threatened to call my dad if we didn't speed things up." The group laughed. "My man was one of a kind." He placed the scorecard in the hole and respectfully shook Dr. Sanderson's hand.

Dr. Sanderson put his hand down in the hole one last time before burying the mementos under loose dirt and rock. Kneeling over the filled-in hole, he removed his baseball cap and asked the group to join him in prayer.

"Heavenly Father, I know that you and Ty are looking down upon us today. Thank you, Lord, for bringing us together on this mountain to honor you and to thank you for the gift of time spent with Ty Bauman Sanderson. While I will always be grateful to have been his father on earth, I know that he is truly your son and is at home in your heavenly kingdom. Thank you, Lord, for the many blessings you have bestowed upon us. In your name we pray—"

They said "Amen" in unison.

Ty's dad remained kneeling in silence, looking at the ground, clearly trying to regain some composure. Hunter couldn't imagine how difficult that prayer had to have been and wondered whether Dr. Sanderson genuinely believed that God was Ty's true father, that he had basically been lent to the Sanderson family for his time on earth. That last part was a hard concept for Hunter to wrap his head around. This whole series of events had put Hunter's already strained faith to further test. Although he had always considered himself a Christian, he was by no means a scholar of the Bible. His own trials and tribulations with self-doubt and depression made him question a lot of the "truths" that others seemed to take for granted. Despite the ups and downs, he did still believe, and he sincerely admired Dr. Sanderson for his courageous display of faith in the worst of times.

Without saying another word, Dr. Sanderson returned the cedar chest, now half empty, to his pack, shouldered it, and started a slow walk down from the peak.

Cole was the first to break the silence: "Time to move, boys."

The rest of the group shouldered their packs, sipped some water, and took one last look at the breathtaking view.

Hunter was the last to leave the burial site. He put his hand down on top of the loose rock and dirt, closed his eyes, and pictured his best friend standing there beside him. "I know you're here, man. This is your place."

"You comin', brother?" Cinco called.

"Yes, sir. Just saying good-bye one more time." Hunter stood up and quickly closed the gap between the two of them.

Cinco put his arm around his neck once he had caught up. "You know he's here," he said. "He wouldn't have missed this deal."

Hunter smirked and nodded. "It's time to get off of this mountain and get fucked up." He had sweated out his hangover, but his head still hurt, and he knew that the only cure was the proverbial hair of the dog that had bit him.

Although it was not nearly as challenging as the hike up the mountain, the trip down had its difficulties. It didn't take long for Hunter to sweat through his clothes for a second time, struggling to keep his hefty frame from accelerating too fast down the steep incline. When it came to the shale, it was downright treacherous. Every step created a miniature landslide, sending loose rock downhill while failing to provide any solid footing.

"Oh, shit!" Cole yelled. He'd lost his footing and slid down quite a ways on his backside about fifty yards below where Hunter had stopped for a breather.

"Safe!" called Jack, who was downhill from the big ranch hand.

"You alright, son?" Dr. Sanderson hollered up.

"Yes, sir. I'm good." Cole's voice revealed a hint of embarrassment as he popped up from his prone position. Seeing Cole go down reminded Hunter of his earlier spill and scraped-up knee, and he tried to be a little more cautious as he made his way down.

Below Hunter and Cinco, Chris had discovered a new technique for getting down the mountain. His knees bent, he was hopping from side to side as if he were downhill skiing. He fell backward every four or five hops, but he was making good progress, sliding substantial distances on every landing.

"Attaboy!" Cinco called out, catching Chris's descent on his iPhone from above. "Get after it!"

Once they were through the shale, the remainder of the descent was relatively uneventful. Hunter's legs were grateful to be back on the flat trail leading back to the parking lot. The rest of the group had beaten him and Cinco to the bottom and were huddled around Stacy's Suburban, beers in hand, relaxing from the grueling hike.

"You boys make it down all right?" Chris asked. "We were about to send out the search party."

Still huffing and puffing, Hunter managed to get out, "Get me a cold beer."

A cold Coors Light never tasted so good. He felt a mixed sense of accomplishment and relief that the hike was over as he sat down on a rock wall that faced the parking lot. Through the loud banter and bullshitting, no one seemed to notice his complete withdrawal from the conversation. The battles with depression had inspired a unique appreciation for good times. It certainly wasn't mania—he was pretty sure it wasn't bipolar disorder he was suffering from— but a subtler, calm feeling. It was the peace of mind that he searched so desperately for. It came so rarely that he had developed a profound appreciation for times such as these. He was content to not say a word, to take it all in and enjoy the moment.

But the moment faded when Dr. Sanderson announced that it was time to pack up for the hot springs. It was already the middle of the afternoon, and they were burning daylight. Ty had always described his dad as having attention deficit disorder, that he was always on the go, and he was living up to that reputation. Hunter smiled as he thought about how the apple hadn't fallen too far from the tree.

CHAPTER 10

PETEY AND THE HOT SPRINGS

The group loaded up into the two vehicles and pulled out of the parking lot, heading north. Cinco rolled down all four windows in the truck to let the cool afternoon air flow through the cab as Hunter cranked up the volume of the stereo to the original version of Robert Earl Keen's "The Road Goes on Forever." Although he enjoyed the many versions recorded thereafter, by the likes of Willie Nelson, Joe Ely, and several live versions by Robert Earl Keen himself and others, nothing, in Hunter's mind, could top the version cut on the album *West Textures*. Hunter particularly liked the fact that there was still a fiddle in the mix on the original version, an instrument that Robert Earl Keen no longer included in his band since the departure of Bryan Duckworth, his best friend since childhood. Regardless of the version, everyone in the truck knew the words of the song by heart and couldn't help singing along as they enjoyed the ride.

The caravan came to a stop at Panther Junction, the park headquarters, and turned east, following the signs pointing toward the hot springs. Hunter opened another Coors Light and looked outside his window at the endless desert terrain. It was hard for him to believe that they had climbed higher than seven thousand feet among tall pine trees in this same country.

"Man, this is a special place." He looked over at Cinco, who smiled.

"I thought we'd lost you, bud," Cinco said. "You got pretty quiet over there."

Hunter took a long pull from his beer. "I'm here," he said, "just catching my second wind. I've been drunk, hungover, and sober again all this morning. Time to repeat the cycle and get drunk again."

The trucks drove for another thirty minutes, at which point they turned right, onto a gravel road, directed by yet another sign for the hot springs. Several hundred yards down, there was a big roadside sign that read, The consumption of alcoholic beverages prohibited beyond this point.

Jack was the first to comment from the backseat: "Fuck that! That's not going to work for this group."

Hunter laughed. "What kind of fucked-up place is he taking us that you can't have a beer?"

The Suburban slowed to a crawl and navigated a sharp turn on an increasingly narrow path, with a solid rock wall on the right and a sheer drop-off to the left. The road had clearly been cut from a rock face. The drop-off was probably only between eight and ten feet to the bottom, but that was high enough to total a vehicle and put a hurt on anyone who attempted to take the curves too fast.

Hunter made a mental note to be extra careful on the way out if he ended up driving.

Several cars lined the wide dirt parking lot at the end of the road. The remnants of a building stood on a hill to the right of the lot, and another one—an old stone building in somewhat better shape—was to the left. Hunter could tell they were close to the river, because there were palm trees and substantially more green foliage than anywhere else in the park.

Dr. Sanderson and his crew had already begun undressing in the parking lot, switching from pants to shorts. Although there was still a chill in the air, the sun was beyond its highest point, and it was warm enough for shorts and short-sleeve shirts. Cinco kept all of the windows in the truck down and left the stereo playing Robert Earl Keen's "Gringo Honeymoon" as he began to get changed.

"How close are we to Boquillas?" Hunter asked. The song, which was written about a trip to the Mexican border town on the other side of the river from the park, had triggered the question.

"We've got to be pretty fuckin' close to the river crossing from here," Chris answered.

Cinco poked his head up over the bed on the far side of the truck. "They shut it down after 9/11, boys. No more gringo honeymoons."

Hunter was now completely apprehensive about any further expeditions into Mexico. He shook his head. Nothing good stayed the same.

With their bathing suits, sunglasses, soft-sided coolers, and even the homemade washer pits, the group looked like they were heading to the beach—if you ignored the hiking boots. A family of five leaving the hot springs met them halfway along the walk and gave them an unfriendly glare as they passed, undoubtedly noticing that everyone in their group was carrying an open beer.

Hunter tried to go out of his way to say, "Hey!" to the two adults and three children, but they hurried past, refusing to make eye contact with him. He laughed. They must have been the owners of one of the vehicles with out-of-state plates in the parking lot.

Once they arrived at the springs, Hunter wasn't sure whether to be disappointed or not. It wasn't exactly what he had pictured, although having never been to a hot springs before, he didn't know whether his expectations were in line with reality. Directly on the bank of the Rio Grande River, these hot springs were contained within a square rock wall that was no more than twenty feet in width. The crystal-clear water flowing in the river was much prettier than the murky springs, but Hunter could still see the bottom, which appeared to be only a couple feet deep.

Three other people were sitting in the hot springs, which was a surprise, given the number of cars in the parking lot. Hunter eyed the trio with curiosity. There were two young women, probably a little younger than their group, sitting noticeably close to a guy who looked even younger. He looked like he was in good physical shape and sported short brown hair and a three-day beard. One of the women, a blond who was slightly pudgy—not a big girl but not slender either—looked both infatuated with the guy and equally irritated with the new company. The girl sitting to the guy's left had her dark hair pulled back, revealing a very light brown complexion. She looked like she might have had a bit of Asian ancestry. From the half of her body that Hunter could see exposed above the water, she looked good in the bright-red bikini she was wearing.

She must have sensed Hunter's gaze, because she made eye contact and greeted the group with a somewhat seductive, "Howdy, guys! The water is awesome."

"Good, because we came to party." Nelson pulled off his shirt and stepped into the water, wearing his brand-name bathing suit, which was cut a little too short for Hunter's taste.

Chris, also shirtless, had tied a Texas-flag bandana around his head and was wearing his aviator sunglasses. He offered the trio a beer from the soft cooler he was carrying.

Although her two companions hadn't quite warmed up to the new arrivals yet, the girl wearing the red bikini responded with an enthusiastic, "Hell, yes!" which got a laugh out of the rest of the group. Chris's gesture was soon appreciated by all, as she stood up to reach for the three beers, revealing the rest of her remarkably fit frame and a small Chinese-letter tattoo in the square of her back.

Hunter chose not to remove the long-sleeve T-shirt he was wearing for fear of sunburn, yet another side effect of the medication he was trying to adapt to. As a kid, he would tan as dark as a Mexican during the summers spent at South Padre Island or playing baseball, but now, he burned after any prolonged exposure to the sun. There were very few clouds in the sky now, and he knew that he needed to be careful with the sun reflecting off of the water as well.

As he sat in the warm pool, Hunter asked, "So where are y'all from?" The question was directed more at the sexy girl than at the other two.

"Austin," she said, looking at her traveling companions. "We came down for a few days to get away."

"That's a long getaway!" Cole said. "Just the three of you?"

"We had heard about Big Bend," the girl said, "and wanted to come out here for an adventure. Three good friends sleeping under the stars. What brings all of you out here?"

Hunter looked at Dr. Sanderson, giving him an opportunity to respond, which he did not.

"Saying good-bye to an old buddy," was all he was willing to say. He felt offering a deeper explanation would somehow cheapen the pilgrimage.

Although clearly annoyed that the new group had stolen the attention of their friend, the other two finally broke their silence and half-heartedly joined the conversation, which seemed to be getting louder by the minute. After an initial round of beers, Jack and Cinco set up the mobile washer pits, and the betting from the night before picked up again, with Nelson hopelessly digging himself into a deep hole.

The hot springs themselves were less than impressive, but Hunter once again disengaged from conversation to take in the beauty of their surroundings. Some might not appreciate it, but they were drinking cold beer on the banks of the Rio Grande on a glorious January day in West Texas. The only way it could get much better would be for Ty to be with them.

"It looks like we've got company, boys," Cinco said, looking across the river. The news that somebody in Mexico was watching them abruptly stopped any conversation. Boy's Town Acuña fresh in his memory, Hunter was instantly on guard. It had only been two nights ago that he and Cinco had had their brush with death by unknown paramilitaries with submachine guns. He could see the same alarm in Cinco's face as they surveyed the activity across the river.

The initial sense of fear turned to curiosity as a barefoot boy no older than ten rode a donkey toward the river. There were a couple of older men standing back in the reeds and the brush, obviously encouraging him to cross. The boy dismounted and rolled up his jeans. The group watched silently as he carefully made his way across the river, shouldering a backpack and fighting the current on what appeared to be not entirely stable footing. When he made it to the north bank, Cinco was waiting for him, offering a helping hand to pull him up out of the river.

"Buenos tardes. ¿Cómo te llamas?" he asked.

The boy smiled and replied, "Petey."

Cinco shook his hand. "Mucho gusto, Petey."

Petey pulled a series of wire sculptures from his backpack, mostly scorpions, but there were a couple of roadrunners as well. Cinco closely examined one of the scorpions. "¡Qué bueno!" he said. "¿Cuánto cuestan?"

The boy looked at him funny and replied, "Cinco."

Cinco asked again, "¿Por todo?" gesturing to the entire inventory.

"No, señor, por cada."

Cinco took forty dollars out of his wallet and handed it to Petey, more than paying for the six sculptures the boy had in his bag.

With an enormous smile, Petey tucked the cash into his pocket.

"¿Tienes más?" Cinco asked, wanting to know if there were more sculptures where those came from.

"¡Sí, señor!" Petey continued smiling as he closed his backpack and quickly headed back across the river.

Cinco passed the wire sculptures around to the group, who all seemed to greatly admire the primitive works of art. Hunter thought of his godson, Ty Junior, who would surely someday appreciate a roadrunner crafted out of fence wire.

Chris seemed to be particularly enamored with the sculptures, and shouted out his encouragement: "¡Córrele, Petey! ¡Quiero más!"

About twenty minutes later, Petey started his trek back across. The group, including the three strangers from Austin, cheered him on, which he seemed to appreciate. All but Dr. Sanderson and Cole had left the hot springs to meet him on the north bank. It was like crossing the finish line at a major marathon when he finally made it ashore. Before opening up his backpack and selling his loot, he had to give everyone a high five. He then took five more sculptures and three Corona beers from his backpack.

Cinco had a hundred-dollar bill in hand, prepared to buy whatever the boy was selling. He handed the bill to wide-eyed Petey and took possession of the sculptures and beers one by one.

"Y'all want a hot Corona?" he smiled and passed around his purchased items.

Hunter, who had already laid claim to a wire roadrunner, had another idea for their newfound friend. "We need a picture with that donkey," he said.

Cinco asked Petey in Spanish if he would mind getting a picture with all of the hombres and his burro.

Petey seemed to be enthusiastic about the request and started back across the river. Chris was the first one to begin wading across, followed by Hunter and Cinco. Dr. Sanderson, Cole, and Jack stayed behind, watching from the hot springs. Hunter crossed barefoot and struggled to keep his footing on the sharp, algae-covered rocks, one hand used for balance and the other trying in vain to keep river water out of his beer. Chris apparently gave up on walking and was on his belly, half-floating and half-sliding over rocks. Once they got to the other side, the footing was even worse, because the entire bank was loose rock. Hunter was absolutely certain he was going to sprain an ankle as he fumbled his way toward the burro.

"We've got to be breaking so many international laws right now." Chris's tone didn't seem overly concerned.

Hunter laughed at his old college roommate, who was drenched from the river. "Man, we're officially wetbacks!"

Chris mounted the donkey and turned him with Petey's help to face Dr. Sanderson's camera. The other two surrounded Petey, who was still holding the rope around his burro's neck. Dr. Sanderson was clearly taking a lot of pictures, and the group smiled and shouted harassment back across the river to Jack, who was apparently too pretty to be a wetback.

When Dr. Sanderson signaled that he was done taking pictures, Cinco handed Petey yet another hundred-dollar bill and said, "Muchas gracias, Petey." He shook the young man's hand and wished him a good day in Spanish.

Petey looked like he was about to explode with excitement. He turned his donkey back toward the brush, where the older men waited for him. Hunter hoped the men were his relatives and not just using Petey to sell goods. They waved to the three Texans and shouted, "Gracias."

Chris was the first one back across, and he was waiting for the others at the edge of the bank. "We just made their year," he said and waved to Petey one last time. He started laughing. "Cinco doubled Petey's annual income in one transaction."

The cold waters of the Rio Grande made the hot springs feel even better to Hunter, who placed the soft-sided cooler within arm's reach of the spot he chose to sit in. "I think I'm good right here for the rest of the afternoon." He opened another beer and sank a little lower in the water.

"Don't get too comfortable, boys," Dr. Sanderson said. "We've got dinner reservations at the Gage at eight." He began putting his hiking boots back on.

"What time is it, man?" Hunter asked Jack, the only one wearing a watch.

"Five on the dot, my man."

Hunter wanted to stay put for as long as they could, but he also knew that it would take over an hour to get to the Gage Hotel in Marathon. It took over an hour to get anywhere out there.

Two more rounds of beers, some mildly interesting conversation with the trio from Austin, and the sun was starting to set up river. Apparently, the two girls were tired of camping, so the three of them were going to roll into Old Mexico for a cheap hotel via the Presidio crossing. Hunter and Cinco warned them about the dangers of the border, but they didn't seem too concerned. Without much of a warning, the three got up from the hot springs, put on their shoes, and started walking back to the parking lot. It was obvious that the guy and the blond-haired girl had wanted to leave for some time.

Hunter called out, "Good luck!" The girl in the red bikini turned and winked at him. Her strut away was well orchestrated.

"That girl is hot, and she knows it," Cinco commented.

"Strippers, man." Jack sounded confident that he knew their story.

"I don't know, but I wouldn't mind being in that dude's shoes tonight," Cole said. "I mean, those aren't your average good buddies."

Dr. Sanderson returned from a walk downriver and was clearly ready to go. "My car is rolling," he said. "Y'all ready?"

Almost in unison, the group responded, "Yes, sir," and started to get up from their seats in the hot springs. Hunter realized he had developed a pretty decent buzz over the course of the afternoon. He had no desire to leave, but knew it was time. Missing dinner would be the least of their concerns if they spent any more time drinking beer in the hot springs.

A somewhat somber mood fell on the group. Hunter sensed that, like him, no one wanted to leave or have the day end. Nevertheless, they all quietly put their boots back on, cleaned up their trash, and started the walk back to the parking area.

"You drivin', man?" Hunter asked. He and Cinco were trailing the rest of the group.

"Yeah, I'm good, bud."

Cinco's response prompted Hunter to open another beer and start singing aloud the lyrics of "I'll Take the Whiskey (You Take the Wheel)," a song written by cowboy-turned-songwriter Chris Wall.

They found themselves yet again trailing Dr. Sanderson away from the hot springs. As they approached the main park road, Hunter noticed the sign they'd seen earlier on the other side of the road, advising that alcohol was prohibited in the park. "Hang on, man," he said. "We need a picture."

Cinco stopped the truck in the middle of the lane.

"What the fuck are we doing?" said Jack from the backseat.

Hunter pointed to the road sign and ordered everyone to get a full beer.

"I see where this is going." Chris was already halfway out of the truck.

"Time to shotgun a beer, boys." Hunter positioned himself next to the sign and instructed Jack to set his camera up on the back of

Cinco's truck to shoot on a timer. The other three gathered around, everyone making sure they didn't block any of the words on the sign. With full, unopened beers in hand, they waited for Jack's signal. Once he had the settings correct, he hit a button and yelled, "Go time," as he ran to join them.

They had already cut holes in the bottom of their cans with knives, so Jack had to quickly catch up. Almost in sync, the four of them popped the top on their beers and put the newly cut holes to their mouths. Chris was the first to be done, and he made it known by slamming the empty beer can to the ground.

Hunter ended up with half of his beer on his T-shirt. "I might need a do-over."

Jack and Cinco were being more careful, taking their time to down their beers.

"Sharp, did you get any of that beer in your mouth?" Chris laughed.

Hunter had never been any good at chugging or shotgunning anything, so he wasn't overly surprised with the result of his efforts.

They all had a good laugh as they previewed the picture from the back of Jack's digital camera. Hunter and Chris opened another beer and climbed back in Cinco's truck to settle in for the hour's drive. Hunter had to hear "Gringo Honeymoon" by Robert Earl Keen once more, this time about twice as loud, and all four of them were singing along at the top of their voices by midway through the song.

About twenty minutes down the road, Cinco pulled the truck over once again. This time, Dr. Sanderson and Cole were waiting for them by the welcome sign to Big Bend National Park. They were sitting in folding chairs, legs crossed, with glasses of wine in hand, like they were at some kind of a picnic.

Cinco rolled down his driver's side window, "¿Qué pasa?"

Dr. Sanderson, who looked really comfortable, replied, "Get out and enjoy this beautiful West Texas sunset, boys."

Hunter had been too wrapped up in the music to notice it, but the sunset was incredible. It had almost completely set by the time they got out of the truck and poured themselves a glass of wine, but the combination of brilliant pinks and oranges appearing to explode into rays extending from the horizon had the entire group in awe.

"God, this place is beautiful," he said.

"God's country, bud." Cinco raised his glass, toasting Hunter's comment.

The group looked somewhat out of place in the desolate high-desert country, sitting around and sipping wine on an asphalt shoulder of the highway, still in their bathing suits from the hot springs, wearing hiking or cowboy boots, felt western hats and baseball caps. They strongly resembled a team of rodeo clowns.

"Look at this ragtag group," Jack said.

"They're going to be really impressed with us at the Gage," Cinco responded with a dry, sarcastic tone.

By the time they finished their wine and got back on the road, the sky had darkened. The absence of any city lights for as far as the eye could see ensured total darkness. It was a clear night, though, and Hunter was convinced that he had never seen so many stars look so bright in a night sky. Everything about this country appealed to him, even the nighttime skies.

The glass of wine and another beer in hand had Hunter on the fine line between feeling very good and being passed out and missing the rest of the night. The hangover, the hike, the day in the sun, the tiring impact of his medication, and quite possibly the last four or five hours of pounding beers had left him feeling a little sleepy. He rolled down his window to get some fresh air.

"Hang in there, bud," Cinco said. "We've got a long night ahead of us."

The crisp January night air felt great and did the trick to slightly wake him up. "Needed a little air," he said. "I'm good."

CHAPTER 11

THE GAGE

Small houses and mobile homes surrounded by fences made of old, rusted metal piping were the first signs of civilization, if you didn't count the lone Border Patrol agent at the checkpoint south of town. Marathon didn't look like much until you got back to the highway, which also happened to be Main Street. They turned left onto the main drag and passed the few shops and the TransPecos Bank prior to seeing the Gage. The historic hotel encompassed an entire city block. Bright lights lined the rooftop and the adobe walls surrounding the compound. Compared with the rest of the dimly lit town, the hotel looked like a Christmas tree. The brick front entrance was clearly left over from the original building, and it looked more like an old schoolhouse than it did a hotel. Further accentuating its Old West appearance was its name—*Gage Hotel*—spelled out on top of the building in enormous block letters. Much to the surprise of the boys in the truck, the limited parking spots in front of the facility and all of the roadside spots on the shoulder of the highway were taken up by vehicles of every kind, from every part of North America.

"Happenin' night in Marathon," Cinco muttered as he pulled the truck over on the shoulder a block west of their destination.

Inside, Hunter fell in love with the hotel. Walking into the lobby was like walking back in time, a time all young Texans romanticized at some point in their lives. There were relics of western life all over the interior. Old saddles and mounted deer hung on the walls alongside famous pieces of western art. Above the ornate fireplace hung a western painting Hunter recognized, but he could not place the artist. A mountain lion was mounted in a stalking posture, perched on a table between two antique chairs in the small sitting area. From the solid wood beams of the ceiling hung an enormous wrought iron circular chandelier. The antique hardwood floors creaked with every step of their boots.

A very friendly Hispanic girl behind the modest front desk greeted them as though they didn't look like drunk bums, but Hunter was somewhat embarrassed by his appearance. Something about western boots, a bathing suit, long-sleeve T-shirt, and grey felt hat didn't feel right in the lobby of what appeared to be a very classy hotel.

Cinco made the arrangements for their room while Hunter sat down and read a brochure detailing the history of the hotel. A rancher by the name of Alfred Gage built the hotel in 1927. The current owner, a successful oil man by the name of J. P. Bryan, stumbled across the old hotel while looking for a house in Marathon, close to one of his nearby ranches. Mr. Bryan completely restored the hotel and has since made a name for himself as a Texas historian, not only because of his family ties to Stephen F. Austin but also through many of his own accolades, including being appointed to the Texas Historical Commission by then-governor George W. Bush. He had successfully turned this historic old hotel in the middle of nowhere into a resort destination that often hosted weddings and events within its quaint confines. Although the Gage managed to maintain its historic atmosphere, it also featured some modern-day amenities, including a spa, a swimming pool, and a world-class restaurant.

Cinco motioned to follow him upstairs to their room, and Hunter picked up his bag and slung it over his shoulder.

"Communal bathrooms, bud." Cinco pointed out the men's restroom down the hallway from their room.

"You kidding me?" Hunter laughed, thinking Cinco really was joking.

"Some have 'em and some don't. Ours doesn't. If you want to pay an extra couple hundred, you can stay out in the suites in the courtyard."

Hunter shrugged. "I mean, man, doesn't bother me."

No different from the rest of the hotel, their room was like a scene from an old western movie. The two twin bed frames were wrought iron, an old pair of chaps hung beside one of the beds, and even more pieces of western art covered the walls.

"I told you this place was cool," Cinco said as he sat down on his bed and started to remove his boots.

"You were right about that." Hunter sat down as well and pulled off one of his own boots. "This place is awesome."

Chris's voice came from the room next door: "Is that you, boys?"

Not only were the walls paper thin, but there was a small window below the ceiling on the wall between the two rooms. It hinged downward, and a chain held it from falling completely open.

"Good thing they provide earplugs." Hunter picked up the plastic bag from the nightstand next to his bed and read that they were actually intended to block out noise from a train that passed through town nightly. "I don't want to hear Nelson jerking off all night."

"I heard that, Sharp. You boys ready for a group shower?"

Hunter looked at Cinco, who was already in a Gage monogrammed robe. "There better be stalls, because I'm not showering with that fuckin' guy."

Whereas the four of them were staying in the main hotel, Dr. Sanderson had booked two of the Los Portales suites, out in the courtyard, for himself and Cole. The more spacious quarters outside the hotel came with private bathrooms and even their own fireplaces.

They didn't have much time to get showered and ready for dinner. Hunter and Cinco were the last ones in and therefore the last ones out of the showers, an unfortunate circumstance, given that there was very little hot water. At least, Hunter thought, the shower sobered him up a bit. Once they were back in the room, they both put on now well-worn jeans, their least-wrinkled button-down shirts, felt hats, and boots and headed downstairs to catch up with the rest of the group.

Hunter and Cinco found them in the White Buffalo Bar, the hotel's cantina, which was named for the enormous white buffalo mounted on the interior brick wall. To get there, they had to exit the front of the hotel and walk next door, through an iron gate, and into an adobe-walled courtyard. The courtyard was part of the restaurant, and despite the cold, there were a few dinner parties eating outside, kept warm by butane heaters and a well-built fire in an outdoor fireplace.

The White Buffalo was cozy, to say the least. There was just enough room for three small, round tables and chairs, and the bar, set in the corner with its white stone base and rustic, dark-wood finish, was long enough for three bar stools. The dark wooden beams on the ceiling, spaced a few feet apart, looked like weathered cedar fence posts and added to the Old West cantina feel. A blazing fire in the stone fireplace gave off plenty of warmth.

"This place keeps getting cooler by the minute," commented Hunter as he and Cinco stepped inside from the courtyard.

Their group was standing around the bar, watching an NFL playoff game on the small flat-screen TV hung behind the bartender. They all turned their heads to see who had come in, and Hunter and Cinco were greeted with an obnoxiously loud "Heeeyyy!"

Dr. Sanderson, who was the only one sitting at a table, anxiously stood up, as if to greet them, but then walked toward the restaurant next door. "Boys, get yourselves a cocktail," he said, "and then it's time to grab our table."

Hunter stepped up to the bar and ordered a Cuba libre, and Cinco ordered a single-malt Scotch on the rocks. As soon as the drinks were poured, Cole led the group back toward the restaurant, where Dr. Sanderson had gone. The dark-haired hostess took them back to a private room adjacent to the hotel lobby. Dr. Sanderson sat at the head of a long, rectangular dark-wood table that could have easily seated twenty. The table was nearly as big as the room, making it somewhat difficult to navigate, particularly for the waitstaff.

"I advised the hotel that it would be in their best interest to separate this group from their other guests at dinner." Dr. Sanderson smiled and gestured for the five of them to take their seats.

"Good call on that one," Jack said, sitting to the right of the doctor. "I can't take these guys anywhere."

As soon as everyone was seated, a middle-aged waitress appeared from the door leading into the restaurant. She was a good-size woman, not necessarily overweight, with long, dark hair and rimmed glasses that made her look like a schoolteacher or librarian.

"Good evening, gentleman. Is everybody good on your drinks? Would you like to look at a wine list?" Her Eastern Bloc accent apparently caught everyone's attention, because conversation came to a halt.

"Yes, ma'am." Dr. Sanderson reached out to take the leather-bound list from her. "We'll need a wine list."

"My name is Olga. Let me know if you need anything."

"Where are you from?" Jack asked.

Olga smiled. "Czech Republic."

Her answer led to further questioning about how she got to Marathon, Texas. She explained that she was a self-proclaimed nomad and had drifted to West Texas. Five years ago, she had taken up temporary residence in a local hostel and, for no apparent reason, had decided to stay. Or at least she hadn't left yet.

While Olga filled everyone's glasses with much-needed water, Dr. Sanderson ordered three bottles of red wine for the table: a six-year-old Silver Oak Cabernet, from Napa, that Hunter noticed on the menu was two hundred dollars a bottle. When Olga leaned over to fill Cinco's glass, her massive cleavage drew everyone's attention on Hunter's side of the table.

Hunter downed his water and looked over the menu, which could have easily been out of any five-star restaurant in downtown San Antonio.

"Damn, this looks good," Cole said.

"This was Ty's favorite restaurant in the world," Dr. Sanderson commented.

Hunter knew that was a tremendous statement from a friend who had, in fact, dined all over the world.

The wine came out and was nearly gone by the time Olga came back to take their food orders. The problem with red wine for Hunter was that he could never sip it; he enjoyed it so much that it tended to go down like water. He was a self-proclaimed wino, and although he appreciated the taste of a good wine, quality wasn't usually a factor in his consumption rate.

Apparently seeing that the wine was disappearing faster than poor Olga could squeeze herself around the table to refill the glasses, Cinco stood up to raise his in a toast. The loud banter came to a halt as he thanked Dr. Sanderson for organizing the trip and bringing them together. With several cheers of "¡Salud!" everyone around the table drank to their friend's father.

The menu had a Southwest Texas flavor and included cabrito, quail, venison, traditional Tex-Mex dishes, and various cuts of prime steak. It all looked good to Hunter, but he couldn't resist the quail as a starter, even though it was actually listed as an entrée on the menu, and the rib eye as his main course. Quail was, by far, his favorite fowl, both to hunt and to eat. Scaled, or blue, quail, the West Texas variety, were difficult to hunt. The native birds were known for running long distances prior to flushing, to the dismay of many pointing dogs. He couldn't tell the difference in taste between bobwhites and blues—both were delicious—but the blues were bigger birds and had more meat.

He ordered his steak medium rare, which, in his opinion, was the only way to eat a steak of any decent cut; to cook it any more was wasting a good piece of meat. Beth used to order her steak well done, which would always prompt Hunter to suggest beef jerky as an alternative.

By the time the food arrived, the table had gone through another three bottles of wine. The volume of their banter had increased to the point that Hunter worried that the guests in the restaurant next door would start to take notice. Even Dr. Sanderson, who, up until this point in the trip, had managed to remain somewhat sober, started to get loose on the seemingly bottomless glasses of vino being poured. He even joined in on verbally abusing Jack, who, more than anyone else, showed signs of wearing down from the afternoon of drinking. Although most of what he said made little sense, he managed to tell a story about his prowess as a junior-high basketball player and how the "brothas" back home in Austin "loved" him. Jack was neither athletic nor tall; an expected and appropriate barrage of insults and snide comments ensued.

Soups and salads came out first, and, although everyone was clearly hungry, the noise level only slightly subsided. Having this gregarious group of high-school buddies and college fraternity brothers all together in one room with a lot of booze had led to increasingly embellished storytelling; even Hunter was having a hard time distinguishing the bullshit from reality. The more wine consumed, the racier and more vulgar the stories became, some of which involved Ty. Hunter was pretty sure that Dr. Sanderson had never heard most of them.

He reminisced about the Sandersons' back house in San Antonio prior to college: "We used to call that house the butt hut! We would sneak girls back there, hopin' to get a blow job."

Cinco smiled widely. "Courtney Wilson."

The two of them simultaneously broke out into laughter. They had all, including Ty, hooked up with Courtney Wilson in the "butt hut" at some point throughout high school.

"She may have fucked Ty," Cinco said proudly, "but I was her first BJ, in eighth grade."

"Real fuckin' accomplishment, buddy," Hunter said. "What's she up to these days?"

"Married with three kids," Cinco responded, still grinning from ear to ear, which had everyone at the table laughing.

Not to be outdone, Dr. Sanderson countered with some college stories of his own that rivaled them all. He told of spending a month during a semester at the University of Texas surfing in the Yucatán. He and a fraternity brother drove down for a weekend and decided not to go back for a full four weeks. Prior to the days of cell phones and caller ID, they were able to convince their parents that they were hard at work in Austin while they were actually living cheaply on the Mexican economy. When their cash ran out, they returned to Austin and back to college.

"That's where Ty got it," Chris said. "That explains a lot." Chris, who would have easily fit into the drug culture that surrounded Austin in the sixties when Dr. Sanderson attended college, seemed the most intrigued by the story.

The quail came a few minutes prior to the steak. Hunter, now drunk for the third time in one day and starting to feel particularly loose, realized that it would be an early night if he didn't get something solid in his stomach. He would soon be on the verge of either puking or passing out, and neither one was an acceptable option. The plate actually had two full birds, one fried and one grilled, along with two enchiladas. He had been the only one who ordered quail, and the others' eyes turned to his plate when it was placed in front of him.

Jack, sitting to Hunter's right, demanded, "Sharp, give me a bite of that bird."

Hunter slid the plate closer to Cole, on the other side of him. "Back off," he said. "You're too fucked up to appreciate this."

Jack nodded in acknowledgement, took a drink of wine, and reentered the conversation across the table from him as if he had never left.

More wine accompanied the entrées, which were either rib eye or tenderloin steaks. Although the quail was fantastic, it hadn't sobered Hunter up as much as he had hoped. The dinner's arrival did manage to quiet the group to some degree as they all focused their attention from virtually yelling at one another to inhaling the enormous amount of meat served to the table. Hunter noticed for the first time since they had sat down that music was playing from the speakers set into the ceiling. He recognized the lyrics to be an old Bob Wills tune.

"Bob Wills is still the king, boys," Cole said, quoting a Waylon Jennings song written in tribute to the Texas music legend.

Although no one at the table was sober enough to fully appreciate the meal, they were sure it was spectacular. The combination of the high-quality wine and the perfectly prepared steaks had everyone leaning back in their chairs, rubbing their bellies, and commenting on how fine a dining experience it had been.

Hunter found himself thinking everything in the world seemed okay in this moment. He was too drunk to have any negative rumination or anxieties running through his head, and he couldn't remember a time when he had laughed so much. Laughter had been hard to come by recently, and he had forgotten how good it felt to laugh with his buddies. He knew it would be short-lived, that tomorrow would come with a whole new set of fears and depressive thoughts, aided and abetted by what surely would be a nasty hangover, but things were good in the moment.

Dr. Sanderson had requested the check come directly to him, and Olga delivered it quickly. It was evident that the sixty-something-year-old physician was ready for bed. Everyone at the table, with the exception of Jack, who was too drunk to comprehend what was going on, and Cole, who, as an employee of the family, was used to the routine, insisted on helping pay the bill; but Dr. Sanderson dismissed their offers and thanked them for making the trip to honor his son. It was obvious that his mood had not elevated the way Hunter's had. He had become more somber and tight-lipped toward the end of the evening. It was clear that the wine had caught up to him and triggered an emotional response that he was desperately trying to keep inside.

With his own personal battles, Hunter felt as if he had developed a better insight into reading others' emotions as well. He made eye contact with Dr. Sanderson and said, "You gonna join us for a nightcap in the bar?" The wine gave Hunter the confidence to keep his eyes locked on Dr. Sanderson's eyes, and he felt as though he had pulled him back in.

"Well, Hunter, I guess I could have a whiskey before bed." The response received a roar from the rest of the guys at the table, who may not have realized the impact they had on the father who had lost his son. Hunter could see it in his eyes.

As they all got up from the table to head back into the bar, Hunter lifted the black book that enclosed the check. The total for the six of them had been well over two thousand dollars. He laughed to himself as he thought about all of that good wine wasted on this group of slapdicks, but he knew Dr. Sanderson hadn't batted an eye. The total overindulgence of dinner was the only way Ty would have had it. Hunter couldn't help wondering whether Dr. Sanderson had insisted on paying for good wine because he knew his son was there in the room with them in spirit. Whether he was or he wasn't, his legacy certainly was, and that was something to celebrate.

The party of six, now a complete circus show in Hunter's expert opinion, spilled into the White Buffalo Bar the same way they had left the restaurant: rowdy. Jack was the first to the bar, ordering a round of top-shelf tequila shots. Dr. Sanderson sat down at the only vacant table, next to the fireplace, ordered a whiskey, and gestured for Hunter to join him. Hunter ordered a Coors Light bottle and took a seat at the two-person table.

There were two cowboys—at least they looked the part, with long-sleeve denim shirts, dark blue jeans tucked into well-worn work boots, and felt western hats—sitting behind them. The one closest to them was picking on an acoustic guitar in his lap. His silverbelly hat looked more brown than gray. A dark handlebar mustache completed the ensemble. He looked as authentic a West Texas cowboy as Hunter could imagine.

Dr. Sanderson struck up a conversation with the two men, who revealed that they worked for different ranches. The doctor was acquainted with the owner of one of them. The discussion quickly turned to the drought, its epic proportions, and the devastating effect it had on every aspect of the cowboys' lives. Hunter swore he heard the guitar player say two inches of rain in eighteen months, but he could not fathom how that could be true. The other one talked about how the drought had made it damn near impossible to run cattle or any other grazing livestock, had decimated big game such as mule deer and elk, and how he hadn't seen a covey of quail in he didn't know how long.

Before the troubadour could start a song, Jack delivered the tequila shots to everyone in the bar. He raised his and made a toast, which only half made sense—something to the effect of loving all of the guys in the room and thanking Olga, their wait-ress from dinner, for having "beautiful breasts." Although they were obviously not too excited about the tequila, the two cowboys found the toast entertaining enough and took the shots with the rest of them.

Jack's shot didn't take. Hunter saw it written all over his face as he tipped back his head to try to drink the tequila. To his credit, and maybe because of some of that athleticism that had made him popular with the "brothas" in junior high, he made a beeline for the back door of the bar, which the bartender held open for him, and hung half of his torso over an old fence as the steak he had for dinner and about three hundred dollars' worth of wine splattered into the yard.

Chris, who stood at the bar with other onlookers, had a look of disgust on his face. "You fuckin' douche bag," he yelled. "That's good tequila."

The bartender quickly closed the door, as if to try to give Jack some privacy, and everyone went back to the conversations they were having prior to the show. The buzz in the bar stopped cold when the cowboy in the silverbelly started picking Townes Van Zandt's "Pancho and Lefty." Hunter was too drunk to tell whether the guy was really good or whether everyone was really into the song choice. Either way, several of their group sang along as he played.

"You know any Bobby Keen?" Hunter was loose enough to make requests once the cowboy was done with his first song.

"Who?"

From the puzzled look on his face, Hunter was not optimistic. "Robert Earl Keen?" He thought he had been clear the first time around.

The cowboy took a long pause, still acting as though he wasn't sure what Hunter was talking about, and then failed at trying to hide a shit-eating grin as he started strumming, "The Road Goes on Forever," Keen's signature tune. By the time he had reached the second verse, every one of them was singing along, with the exception of Dr. Sanderson, who, Hunter noticed, was tapping his boots to the rhythm, and Jack, who must have been still trying to compose himself out back.

The cowboy troubadour must have felt that the bar crowd's reaction to his last song was as good as it was going to get. He propped the guitar up in the corner, and he sat back and clearly enjoyed the attention and free drinks being offered to him by Hunter's group of buddies.

"Good one to end on, man." Hunter tipped his glass in a toast, receiving a tip of the hat in return.

"You know, Stacy really likes you, bud." The words out of Dr. Sanderson's mouth caught Hunter completely off guard. Dr. Sanderson sipped his whiskey and fixed his eyes on Hunter, who had hoped this conversation would not come. Despite the booze, Hunter could not escape the intense feeling of discomfort coupled with a strong urge to flee from the table. He struggled for an adequate response, but he couldn't find one in his significantly impaired brain.

He took a long pull from his Coors Light and met Dr. Sanderson's stare.

"Son, I can't tell you what to do, but don't overthink it. Go with your heart. Either way, you're a lot better than that last son of a bitch she dated." Dr. Sanderson smiled, which put Hunter slightly more at ease. He knew Stacy's last boyfriend was not very well liked by the family, and Ty couldn't stand him. He was a smooth fast-talker from the East Coast who in no way fit the Sanderson mold.

"Yes, sir." Somehow, Dr. Sanderson knew that he had a bad habit of overthinking everything. His self-doubt led to constant over-analysis and indecision, often resulting in missed opportunities and disappointment. Hunter had not shared the depth or intensity of this internal strife with anyone, not even Ty, so he was surprised that Dr. Sanderson had read him so well.

"I like her too," Hunter said. "Y'all are like family." As soon as he said it, it occurred to him that Stacy really could be the one for him. She was a cool girl he always had fun with, from a great family he loved, and she was smoking hot. What was there not to like? She'd always been off-limits. Then, as they seemingly always did, the negative thoughts of self-doubt countered the positive: He knew she could do better than him, and she shouldn't have to put up with his bullshit issues.

Dr. Sanderson had apparently discussed this matter as much as he had intended, because he finished his whiskey drink and reached across the table to shake Hunter's hand. "You two would be good together," he said. "Just one old man's advice. Take it or leave it. I'm going to bed. Buenas noches."

Hunter tried to form a serious facial expression and shook the doctor's hand. "Yes, sir. Buenas noches."

Hunter sat cross-legged at the table, watching Dr. Sanderson as he exited the bar and contemplating the heart-to-heart discussion. He was once again lost in thought, completely disconnected from the ruckus happening around him, half excited about the possibilities, and half terrified that he would find a way to fuck it up.

"What the fuck was that about?" Cinco's voice broke through and pulled Hunter's focus outward again. Cinco sat down and slid another Coors Light across the table. "Y'all looked like you were in a pretty intense discussion there for a second."

Hunter took a sip. "Talking about Stacy."

Cinco started to laugh. "That must have been awkward."

The laughter was contagious, and it made Hunter chuckle as he replied, "Yeah, it kind of was." He didn't want to let on that Dr. Sanderson had actually encouraged him to date his daughter.

Olga, who must have been done with her shift in the restaurant, had joined their group at the bar and was shooting some kind of flavored vodka. Jack, still looking a little puny from his tequila episode, was leaning on the bar next to her. From where he sat, Hunter could hear him slurring his words and making very little sense.

"Poor Olga," he remarked to Cinco, who laughed and watched in amusement.

Olga seemed fairly entertained with the attention—either that or she was a really good sport—as she playfully bantered back and forth with their drunk buddy.

"We're going to the compound!" Jack announced to everyone in the bar.

Olga laughed hysterically and corrected him, "The commune."

Jack couldn't be corrected. "Y'all want to go check out that compound?"

Cinco looked at Hunter and shook his head, laughing at Jack's drunken inattention. Chris, who had been standing on the other side of Olga at the bar, intently listening to their conversation, announced he was in as well, and Hunter knew exactly why: Anyone hippie enough to live in a commune would be hippie enough to have some drugs.

"This ought to be interesting," Cinco commented as he got up to follow the other three, who were now walking out the front of the bar.

Hunter turned to Cole and asked, "You in?"

"Shit no. I'll sit right here and drink cold beer until y'all get back."

They walked around the block that was the Gage until Olga pointed out her car, a bright yellow 1980s diesel-engine Mercedes Benz with a multitude of images and sayings painted all over it and a peace symbol for an emblem instead of the traditional Mercedes logo. Surprisingly, it started right up when Olga got in and turned the keys. Cinco looked at Hunter before getting in the backseat and calmly said, "We're all gonna die tonight."

CHAPTER 12

MARATHON HIPPIES

The drive was short; nothing was far in the no-stoplight town. On the way, Olga talked about the virtues of living in her commune. Her passengers remained relatively quiet as she described the "vision" of her "humble abode" and all of the interesting people who pass through. She described their philosophy for living as environmentally friendly and organic, down to the building materials and composting toilets. Hunter had never associated West Texas with hippies, but he had met enough of them on this trip to last a lifetime.

Olga pulled her car up to the clump of small buildings, and her headlights shone on a colorful wooden sign hung between two eight-foot-tall posts that read, La Loma Hostel. The hostel was composed of a series of small adobe buildings connected by a stone pathway. Littered throughout the dirt yard were hand-painted signs with sayings that only someone privy to an inside joke could understand.

The first one that caught Hunter's eye stated, The revolution will not be funded.

Cinco remarked, "What the fuck?" under his breath as the car came to a stop in front of one of the adobe huts.

They were greeted by a party of two men and a woman sitting on a porch in front of the hut. Hunter could barely make them out by the light of a fire inside a tiny clay chimenea, the only light, it seemed, for miles.

"Olga, you brought guests," one of the men said, sounding slightly irritated.

"That's my old man," she said.

"Your dad?" Jack inquired.

Olga laughed again. "No, my boyfriend."

"You have a boyfriend?" Jack sounded disappointed.

Hunter had to get closer to the porch and chimenea to get a better look at the three hippies. They were sitting in old cloth recliners that had clearly spent some time outside in the elements. Olga's boyfriend was, by far, the oldest of the group—at least in his late fifties. He had a well-weathered face, and he'd pulled his silvery-gray hair back into a ponytail. His beard was patchy and unkempt, and he wore vintage cowboy clothes: a colorful pearl-snap shirt, torn jeans, and an old western-cut coat.

The smell of marijuana got stronger as the group approached the porch. Olga's old man had taken a hit of something from a ceramic pipe and passed it to the younger woman sitting in the chair next to him. He then reached for a jug on the porch next to his recliner and took a long swig.

"Y'all blazin'?" Jack asked. "Can I have a hit?" He sounded like an eighteen-year-old frat guy trying to score some pot. His attempt to assimilate backfired; none of the three even acknowledged his presence.

"These guys hiked San Isabel today to bury a friend," Olga said in an obvious attempt to break the ice.

The old man showed no sign of that making an impression, caring about their adventure or their loss of a friend, but the younger couple became more welcoming by saying hello. They looked a lot less like they belonged in West Texas. Although they were clearly younger than their host, they looked somewhat worn and ragged from the road. The woman's straight, dirty-blond hair hung below her ears, and she wasn't wearing makeup or jewelry. Her tight-fitting ripped jeans revealed a small yet athletic frame, and at the hem, they covered up the vast majority of her pointy western-cut boots. She introduced herself as Jean—Jeanine to her family, and Jeany to her husband, Dan, who was now at least making eye contact. Dan was tall and slender, had shaggy dark hair and a full goatee. His untucked flannel shirt looked like it had never been washed.

Hunter noticed a friendliness in Jean's eyes.

"Where are you from?" she inquired with a soft smile.

He explained their story. The couple somehow put Hunter at ease. He didn't know whether it was that they were both stoned out of their minds or whether they were genuinely friendly, but he took an immediate liking to them. He rambled more than what he was accustomed to as they smiled and listened, throwing out the occasional "That's cool!" or "Sorry, man!" as he talked about Ty. They both seemed to genuinely care about what he had to say, which Hunter found to be a refreshing change from most people he came across.

They explained that they had been following a band out of

Oklahoma that Dan managed a website for. The band had a gig in Marfa, and the married couple had split off to spend a few days in Marathon.

"We might stay for a while," Dan explained. "We like it here, and they've got Wi-Fi, so I'm good."

Hunter and Dan quickly discovered that they had similar taste in music, and they compared notes on their favorite Texas-based artists. The only point of contention was when Hunter asserted that Robert Earl Keen was "as good a songwriter as there ever has been," to which Dan replied, "He's no Willie." Jean inserted herself in the argument as she saw fit, arguing both sides convincingly well but ending up siding with her husband.

"Willie's just been doing it longer," she said.

Feeling parched because he had not had a drink in at least twenty minutes, Hunter asked Jean for a taste of whatever was in the jug that was being passed around. She handed it over, issuing a warning to "tread lightly." Hunter laughed and tilted the jug back, taking a full swig of sweet-tasting sangria.

"That's good shit!" He tilted it back again for a second go.

"Whoa, killer!" Jean pulled the jug out of his hands midsip. "That Everclear will fuck you up."

Hunter had always had a thing for girls who could cuss while maintaining a sweet disposition, and Jean was no exception. He found himself liking her more and more as their conversation continued.

Dan and Jean were clearly comfortable around each other; they seemed as much buddies as they were husband and wife. They laughed at each other's jokes, although Hunter didn't get all of them, in part because they were extremely high and he wasn't. Hunter found himself slightly jealous of the relationship they seemed to have, and he hoped that he could someday have the same.

While Hunter was conversing with Dan and Jean, Chris was working the old man. He apparently had made some kind of a connection, because before Hunter knew it, Chris had the ceramic pipe and had passed it on to Jack.

Chris had a way of antagonizing people without them knowing it, and he had clearly fired this man up. The man made some off-hand remark about President Bush and the Republican Party, to which Jack, who was now sitting on the porch, looking confused, had to have taken offense, being that his father was a Republican senator. Jack never revealed who his dad was, nor that any of the political commentary fazed him, despite the old man on the porch all but accusing his family of being warmongers. Jack, instead, seemed to have disengaged from the whole conversation, which he'd never really been a part of, and talked to himself. He was barely conscious to begin with, and the weed may have completely done him in.

Cinco stood over him, looking disgusted with their current set of circumstances. "You ready, Sharp?" He interrupted Hunter midsentence.

Hunter, who felt like he was managing his intoxication level adequately, may have been on the same wavelength as his audience. Either way, he had found their conversation surprisingly entertaining, and he wasn't in a rush to leave.

"Y'all want to come back to the Gage for a nightcap?" he offered.

Jean didn't seem overly excited about the invitation, but Dan shrugged his shoulders and said, "Why not?" Jean offered to drive them back to the hotel, claiming that, although she was clearly high, she was the most sober of the group.

Hunter and Cinco had to help Jack into the back of the couple's old 1980s Ford Bronco. He wasn't passed out and didn't need to be carried, but he was extremely confused and required steering. Prior to being pulled away, he insisted on giving Olga one last hug, which lasted an awkwardly long time. When he started to rest his head on her breasts, Cinco intervened and pointed him to the car.

"Let's go, Nelson. You're done here."

Olga took the whole thing in stride, politely laughing through the entire episode. Her boyfriend didn't seem to be concerned in the least, and he certainly did not make an effort to say good-bye.

The Bronco started right up, and Cinco, sitting between Hunter and Chris in the backseat, commented that he hadn't been in a car like this since high school. Hunter sensed an element of sarcasm in Cinco's comments that he didn't particularly like, given that Dan and Jean had become his new friends and were kind enough to offer them a ride back to the Gage.

"This ride not fancy enough for you, cocksucker?" The thought turned into words faster than he could filter it, clearly a direct result of the wine and Everclear.

Cinco let out a fake laugh and threatened to whoop Hunter's ass when they got back to the hotel. Chris must have found the entire exchange hysterical, because he was giggling like a schoolgirl on the other side of Cinco.

Jean turned up Willie Nelson's "Stay a Little Longer" and ignored what was going on in the backseat.

CHAPTER 13

THE NIGHTCAP

They returned to find Cole in the adobe-walled courtyard of the Gage, sitting around a circular table next to an open fire pit. The White Buffalo Bar had long closed down, and the raging fire he had built accounted for the vast majority of light in the courtyard. A mobile poker table set was laid out in front of him, and he looked anxious to play.

Cinco walked Jack, who had passed out the minute he had gotten into the back of the Bronco, to his room while Hunter pulled up a chair at the poker table. He invited Dan and Jean to sit down, but they chose to stand and watch the game unfold.

"You out here playing by yourself?" It looked to Hunter as if a game had already occurred.

Cole shook his head and took a pull from a Styrofoam cup that Hunter knew had to contain whiskey. "Nah, I played Hold'em with those cowboys from the bar."

Chris sat down on the other side of the ranch hand. "How'd you do, man?"

Cole was still shaking his head. "Those motherfuckers took me for a grand." There was a hint of pain and disappointment in his voice.

"And you want to keep playing?" Chris asked sarcastically.

"Shit yeah. I need to win some money back from you pretty boys."

Although the booze had kept him relatively warm up until this point, sitting outside, despite being next to the fire pit, quickly made Hunter realize that it was extremely cold. The temperature had rapidly dropped, even since they had returned from the commune. He could now see his breath, and he was shaking around like a nervous five-year-old about to piss in his pants.

Cole disapprovingly looked him up and down while shaking his head and matter-of-factly stating, "You need a fuckin' coat." He had been smart or maybe sober enough to remember his Carhartt work coat, which he had buttoned and the collar flipped up to his ears, revealing little of his face between the coat and his gray felt hat.

"Man, it got colder out here," was all Hunter could muster. He turned toward the hotel lobby to retrieve a coat from his room, but Cinco was already coming through the other direction, coat in hand.

"Looking for one of these, bud?"

Hunter was relieved not to have to make the trek up the stairs to the room, half in fear that everyone would go to bed while he was upstairs.

"Yes, sir. I appreciate it."

Cinco tossed the ranch-style work coat toward Hunter. It wasn't quite adequate for the frigid temperature, but it was a lot better than nothing at all. With a little added warmth, he could now focus on the cards being dealt.

The four of them started another Texas Hold'em game in response to Cole's pleas. The ranch hand was almost in as bad a shape as Nelson but bound and determined to win some money back after his apparent shellacking by the cowboys from the bar.

"Bets to you, Cole," Cinco pointed out.

Cole responded to the call without taking his focus off of the two cards in his hand. There was a long silence as he contemplated his next move.

Cinco had put in more chips than Cole had in front of him. Four cards were lying faceup on the table: the ace of diamonds, the eight of clubs, the jack of hearts, and the ace of hearts.

Cole spit tobacco into an empty beer bottle, took a sip of his whiskey, and pushed all of his remaining chips into the pot in the center of the table. The move was clearly a final act of desperation, a last stand.

"Well, let's see what you got." Cinco flipped his two cards, the ace of spades and the three of diamonds, prior to the river card being dealt now that Cole had bet it all.

Cole revealed his cards simultaneously, the ace of clubs and the ten of spades. Chris, who was dealing and had folded earlier in the hand, flipped over the river card: the three of spades.

"Goddamn," Cole muttered under his breath as he pushed away his chair from the table.

"Un-fuckin'-believable. Tough break, man." Hunter could not believe Cole got beat with three aces in his hand.

Cole reached into his lip with his right pointer finger and quickly removed the snuff he had been dipping, pulled down on the brim of his beat-up felt hat, and marched away to his room without saying another word.

"We gave him a shot to get back in it," Cinco said once Cole was out of earshot. He sounded somewhat apologetic.

"That hangover is going to hurt in the morning." Chris looked relieved that he hadn't stayed in on that hand. He collected the cards and passed them over to Cinco.

"Was he okay?" Jean's giggling revealed an element of insincerity in her concern.

Hunter nodded. "He'll be okay. He's used to us taking his money. Ty used to take him in washers and cards all the time. They only fought once, and Cole beat Ty's ass." Hunter laughed out loud thinking of that story. He hadn't been at the ranch for that one, but Cole and Ty joked about it every time they were together after that. Ty had been in high school and got a little cocky after taking Cole's money in a poker game. They were both drunk, and they ended up wrestling more than actually fighting, as the story went. Of course, the actual outcome of the story varied by the storyteller, but Hunter was pretty confident that Cole had put Ty in his place. Without Ty around to beat up on tonight, he was probably in his room, pouting.

Hunter had no idea what time it was, nor did he care. Going to bed would mean having to face the realities of tomorrow: a three-day hangover, an end to the weekend, and, worst of all, the thoughts and depression that would inevitably return in full force. He knew he was nearly blackout drunk, walking that fine line again between passing out in a pool of his own vomit and maintaining a semifunctional state of extreme inebriety. His comfort was in the fact that he didn't have to think.

"Deal 'em up, brother," he said and pushed several chips out to the middle of the table.

"Sharp, we're not going to take your money too," Chris said, counting his chips.

That was not what Hunter wanted to hear. "What the fuck, man? Let's play."

Chris and Cinco ignored Hunter's pleas and exchanged their chips for several hundred dollars from the cash pile.

"Fuckin' pussies," Hunter muttered as he exchanged a much smaller pile of chips than the other two.

Cinco pinched out a dip of snuff and then collected the remainder of the cash from the poker game.

"Calm down, bud. I'll take your money in washers." He stood up slowly and walked over to where they had set up the mobile washer pit.

"That's my boy! I'm in." Hunter grabbed three Coors Lights from an ice chest next to the poker table. His spirits were suddenly lifted with the assurance that he had a partner in crime.

"Time to shotgun a beer," he said. The temperature had dropped again, and the booze would have to supply whatever warmth his coat couldn't. He extended an open hand toward Cinco, as a surgeon demanding a scalpel from a surgical tech might, and said, "Knife?"

Cinco produced a buck knife from his pocket and handed it to the surgeon. Hunter handed beers to Chris and Cinco, whose body language indicated he wasn't overly excited about the prospect of drinking an entire twelve-ounce beer in a single swallow. Hunter carefully pierced his beer with the knife and then cut a rectangular opening about an inch in height and width. Cinco and Chris did the same, although not as carefully or accurately in Hunter's estimation.

"Salud, boys!" Hunter tipped back the brim of his felt hat so it wouldn't get in the way, carefully placed the fresh-cut hole in the can to his mouth, and with his right hand popped the aluminum tab on top. Eleven and three quarter ounces of ice cold beer hit the back of Hunter's throat at once, and he did his best to get it all down in a couple of swallows. Once that was done, he tossed the can and at least a quarter ounce of beer—a typically weak effort on his part—loudly to the ground.

Chris finished his beer nearly simultaneously, but Cinco was clearly struggling. He must have had as much Coors Light on the front of his Carhartt jacket as he did in his mouth, and when he gave up on the lackluster effort, he tossed the can to the ground with a substantial amount of fluid inside, made obvious by the sloshing sound it made when it hit the cement.

While Cinco and Hunter went at it on the washer pit, Chris disappeared outside the adobe courtyard walls of the Gage with Dan and Jean. After what seemed like an uncommonly long game because of their drunken states—a game that Hunter narrowly won—Chris suddenly reappeared with the couple. He looked like he had stolen something and was trying to play it cool.

"Had to make a run back to their car," he claimed, even though he knew everyone knew that they had left the confines of the hotel to smoke weed.

Hunter found Chris's clumsy attempt to cover his pot smoking entertaining. "Everything alright out there?" he asked while laughing.

"Why are you laughing?" Jean asked in a sweet yet puzzled voice. The weed and the booze had apparently taken their toll on her ability to think straight, because she looked as confused as she sounded.

Hunter didn't have the patience or, for that matter, the ability to explain the humor in the situation.

"I'm laughing at that jackass." He pointed at Chris, who gave him the finger and walked by him without looking at him.

"You don't have to be shady, man. Your wife isn't here." Hunter knew that Chris's new bride wasn't fond of his affection for smoking pot.

"If the only bad thing you do on this trip with this group of fuckin' degenerates is smoke," Cinco chimed in, "you deserve a medal, bud."

"I'm going to take you two bitches in washers," Chris said, fishing a beer out of the ice chest. He casually walked over to join them at the washer pit.

Hunter made a point of saying good-bye to Dan and Jean. They announced that they would be walking back to the commune, which Hunter thought was weird, but he realized that they were more fucked up than he was, which, upon reflection, seemed like quite an accomplishment. Hunter tried to give them his phone number, insisting that they come visit him in San Antonio, but he wasn't sure whether that communication got through effectively and, even if it did, whether they were able to accurately input his number into their phones. Jean gave him a long hug and a kiss on the cheek, also insisting that they would come to visit. The entire scene was pretty comical, considering they had known each other for only a few hours. Hunter thought it was odd how, sometimes, he felt more connected to strangers met over beers than to those closest to him.

"Are you done making friends, bud?" Cinco was standing next to

Chris on one end of the washer pit. Chris had made quick work of Cinco and was ready for another challenger.

"I have to throw against this guy?" Hunter responded, pointing at Chris who seemed to be swaying from side to side while sipping on a beer and eyeing the square box that was roughly seven yards away.

He shifted his stare toward Hunter. "This is when I play my best washers, man. Hundred bucks?"

Hunter had enough booze in him to not care how damaging hundred-dollar games of washers could be to his bank account, despite knowing that it would hurt the other two men's pockets significantly less.

"You got it," Hunter said. "Hundred a man."

Cinco observed from the other end of the pit. "Y'all are idiots," he said.

The comment fired Hunter up more. "Hundred a man, bud. You want winner?"

Cinco shook his head. "Whatever. I'll take your money."

This was a victory for Hunter, who held up his hands like he had already won. "Hundred a man! He's in!"

Hunter would come to regret his zeal to raise the stakes, but he was so drunk that it didn't even faze him that he couldn't hit the washer board, much less get close to the hole. His only saving grace was that Chris was as off as he was, resulting in the worst display of competitive washers that any of the three of them had ever seen.

A player's performance at washers, much like that in many games along the lines of pool, darts, and horseshoes, functions on a bell curve when graphed as a function of the quantity of alcohol consumed while playing. Hunter and Chris had found themselves on the declining side of the curve, closer to the trough than the peak. Much to the irritation of Cinco, they also seemed more interested in storytelling than throwing washers. In between throws, they recalled events from their college years, laughing hysterically like two little kids laughing at their own jokes.

Although it would all flood back in the morning, the ability to temporarily forget about the troubles of reality contributed to Hunter's high. He couldn't remember the last time he had felt so at ease and laughed with such abandon. It felt good to be away from the worries of the world out in the middle of nowhere with the guys he felt closest to. As an only child, they were the closest thing to brothers he would ever have, and this trip would no doubt strengthen that bond for years to come. Hunter felt exceedingly close to the peace of mind that he had been relentlessly pursuing.

The first game ended with a narrow win by Chris, or more accurately, a loss by Hunter.

"Double or nothin'!" Hunter was more concerned about everyone going to bed than about the hundred dollars he had just lost or placing another hundred on the line.

Cinco shook his head in disbelief. "Are you fucking kidding me, Hunter? You didn't even hit the board. Don't lose all of your money before I get a run at it."

Hunter went from laughing with Chris to a straight-faced look of disdain toward Cinco. "Give me one more shot," he said. "We're going double or nothin'."

Cinco gestured with his right hand, as if to say, Go ahead, whereas Chris didn't appear to be sober enough to even recognize that he had won a hundred dollars.

The second game went the same as the first. Hunter and Chris cut up—despite the fact that it was a two-hundred-dollar game—more than they focused on throwing washers. Hunter, visibly frustrated by the fact that he could not hit the board even once, was still having a grand time and not showing any sign of slowing down his intake of cold beer. Chris, whose eyes had been barely open for the last couple of hours, somehow managed to pull out another victory.

"Double or nothin'?"

There was no answer this time from Chris.

Cinco intervened. "I think he's done, bud. You probably should be too."

Hunter suddenly realized he didn't have two hundred dollars in cash on him. "I'll get you back in the morning, brother." Chris nodded and disappeared into the hotel.

CHAPTER 14

LET'S FINISH IT

Despite the exodus of all but one of his running buddies, Hunter was still not convinced it was time for bed.

"What time is it, man?" he asked Cinco, who was picking up the washer boards and beers they'd discarded throughout the courtyard.

Cinco pulled out his phone and a painful look fell over his face. "Ten 'til five, bud."

He had just put the last beer can in the trash when the West Texas silence was abruptly broken by the sound of an inbound train horn that seemed to shake the entire hotel. It felt as if the train was bearing down on the two of them right within the walls of the courtyard.

"Holy shit! That'll wake you up." Hunter grabbed two Lone Stars and motioned for Cinco to follow him toward the street. He knew he could guilt Cinco into sharing a final beer with him, regardless of the hour. You didn't let a friend, much less a best friend, drink alone at the end of the night. There was some code somewhere that mandated it. At least that was what Hunter was betting on in the moment.

The train was blowing through town as he walked through the gate and onto the street, which despite the many parked cars at the hotel was completely void of activity. The light from the hotel's roadside marquee sign was the only illumination on their side of Highway 90. On the other side, where the railroad tracks ran parallel to the street, there were red crossing lights, marking crossing gates to the other side of town.

Hunter sat down on the curb, put the two beers to his side on the cement, and rubbed his eyes. He was extremely weary from a lack of sleep. He fixed his gaze on the train running west into the darkness. The tracks couldn't have been more than a hundred yards from where he sat, and he was separated from them only by the highway and an open field. He gave half a second's thought to riding west in one of the cars but came to the realization that running away would only solve half of what troubled him. Jumping the train might allow him to escape the changing world around him, but there was no escaping himself.

Cinco sat down next to him on the curb and twisted the cap off his Lone Star. Neither of them said anything as they watched the last train car disappear into the West Texas wilderness. The red warning lights stopped blinking, and all of the sudden, the only light outside of the hotel was from the brick and wood Gage marquee. Marathon became deathly quiet, a stark contrast to the deafening shrill of the train's horn seconds before.

"It's been a good run, brother." Cinco took a sip of his beer while still staring west into the darkness. "We almost died several times getting out here, but it was every bit worth it."

Hunter, still wrapped up in his thoughts, didn't reply. His earlier high had given way to a sadness triggered by the disappearance of the train and an end to more than the weekend. He felt like he wanted to talk to Cinco about his personal struggles, but he hesitated to do so. He had never felt comfortable revealing his demons, even to his best friends. His fear of being perceived as abnormal or—even worse, weak—prevented him from being honest with anyone about what was going on in his head. This insecurity and lack of transparency had prevented him from fostering meaningful relationships while also doing substantial damage to his existing relationships, including his friendship with Cinco. When things were bad, he rarely called the people close to him, instead choosing to hole up like some hunted outlaw. It was a lonely and, at times, torturous existence.

The silence must have made Cinco uneasy, or at least inquisitive, because he continued to press Hunter into conversation.

"You doin' alright, bud?"

Hunter nodded and sipped his beer. After a long pause, used primarily to gather his thoughts, he turned his head toward Cinco.

"Things are changing, man. Ty's gone. You're fixin' to get married. This could be the last run." Although the changes around him were weighing heavily on his mind, there was clearly more to it than that. Hunter often tried to rationalize the irrational and convince himself that the sources of his troubles were actually external.

"I'm getting married," Cinco said, "not dying." He was almost laughing. "What are you going to do about Stacy?"

Hunter had also been thinking about that. The truth was that he liked her. What was there not to like? Eventually, if she got close, she would see his faults and would certainly not see him the same way she looked at him today. How could she like someone who, at times, found it very difficult to like himself?

"I don't know. I mean, I'll call her when we get back." He knew that he probably wouldn't.

"Don't fuck that up. She's a cool girl."

"Ten four, buddy." Hunter smirked sarcastically as he took another pull from his Lone Star.

Despite the self-doubt, he was somewhat excited about the possibility of a relationship with Stacy. The thought of trying to court her made him anxious; in his mind, there was a really good chance he would fuck it up, but the potential seemed worth the risk. It was something to look forward to and might motivate him to get his shit together. At times like these, even the potential of happiness was enough to keep him going.

"You and Ty are my only brothers. I don't know if I ever got around to telling him that."

It was Cinco's turn to smirk. "He knew that, bud, and we all felt that way. That's not gonna change."

Hunter nodded, despite knowing that things would inevitably, to some degree, change.

"I know you're going through a lot. I don't know exactly what all of it is, but I'm here for you, brother." Cinco's tone had changed from lighthearted to genuine sincerity.

Hunter went silent for several seconds, debating how much he should reveal to Cinco.

"My doc says I have clinical depression."

It was the first time he had told anyone other than his family-practice physician and a consulting psychiatrist. He wasn't quite ready to try to explain all of the crazy shit that accompanied his depression in the form of OCD, but it did feel good to let Cinco in, at least partially, on what was going on.

"How long have you been dealing with that?" Cinco didn't appear to have any judgment in his tone.

"I mean . . . for as long as I can remember."

"Why didn't you tell me?"

Hunter shrugged. "I didn't know what it was until recently, and I don't need anybody feelin' sorry for me."

Cinco looked at him with a concerned expression. "Dude, everybody has issues. I know lots of people that have dealt with depression at some point. It doesn't mean you're not tough. Don't get me wrong, you're fuckin' crazy, but I've always known that."

Hunter laughed. "Yeah . . . don't forget that either."

"You and I will always be brothers. Mia knows that too. We're here for you, bud."

A faded Border Patrol SUV suddenly appeared from the east, slowed down as it passed by, the driver investigating their presence on the side of the road at five in the morning. As they had with the train earlier, they watched the vehicle until its red taillights were out of sight and they were once again surrounded by silence.

Although it was short, the conversation meant a lot to Hunter and completely changed his demeanor. Making Cinco aware of his struggles and not sensing any judgment or distance between them felt like having a tremendous load lifted off of his shoulders.

"Let's grab one more, bud." Cinco must have read his mind. They walked back into the Gage courtyard and took the last two Lone Stars out of the cooler.

"The last two of the weekend. Let's finish it." Hunter handed Cinco a bottle and cocked his in a toasting motion. "Here's to our brother, Ty, for bringing us out here."

Hunter gently tapped the glass longneck to Cinco's, who responded simply, "To Ty."

They drank their beers standing above the glowing embers in the fire pit. Not another word was said; there was nothing else to say. No matter what changes life would bring, this would always be an incredibly special place that would bring them back together for years to come. The trip would become an annual pilgrimage that neither of them would ever miss for as long as they were physically able.

As the sky to the east started to glow with the pinkish orange signs of first light, Hunter said a silent prayer of thanks to the Lord, praising Him for creating this vastly wild and rugged West Texas country, which he was certain was made for men like him and his brothers, Cinco and Ty. This was a place where he felt he could find the peace of mind he continually searched for. One last silent toast to the sky, confident Ty was up there watching, and it was the official end of the journey that would affect his life forever.

READER'S GUIDE

1. What was your overall impression of the book? Did you find it exciting, disturbing, depressing, uplifting, or informative?

2. Did you identify with any particular character or characters?

3. Was the setting a region you find compelling, that you would like to visit? Does it evoke the romance and anarchy of the Old West, or do you see it as desolate and uninviting?

4. What kind of story is this? For example, what kind of movie would be made from this book—a modern western, a road-trip movie, a drinking buddy comedy, a drama about grief?

5. Have you dealt with this sort of grief before, the loss of a close friend? If so, how did you honor that person? Did you perform any sort of group ritual like the trip to San Isabel Peak?

6. Can you identify with Hunter's feelings toward Dr. Sanderson? How would you describe the relationship?

7. Did the amount of drinking and driving affect you in some way? Is this particular to the region or a general aspect of American culture? Is Hunter's justification—that he knows his limits—reasonable and acceptable, dangerous and irresponsible, or simply realistic?

8. Have you had to deal with something you felt you needed to keep secret, like Hunter and his depression? Were your friends as supportive as Cinco was?

9. What did you think of the music in the book? Were you familiar with it, or did you look into any of it? How would you describe the relationship between the music and the setting, the music and the characters?

10. How did you feel about the use of Spanish in the book? Was it effective at conveying a sense of the region? Were you able to understand the conversation, even though most of it wasn't translated?

11. Having read the stories of Alfredo and Gloria—and then, later in the book, Petey—what are your thoughts about illegal immigration and the role of the immigrant in Texas culture?

12. For those of you familiar with Texas, do you feel that the characters from the various cities are representative of those cities' cultures? Does Nelson seem like someone from Dallas, Chris like someone from Houston or Austin, Hunter like someone from San Antonio? What personality traits do you associate with each of these cities?

13. Are you familiar with or have you been to Texas hunting

ranches like the White Ranch or F bar R? This is a big part of Texan culture that only a small percentage of the population has access to. What are your initial impressions from the description of the ranches and the families who own them?

14. Have you ever crossed the border with Mexico or been to another foreign country, and if so, was your experience like Hunter and Cinco's? Could you tell whether the border guards on one side were searching for one type of contraband and those on the other side interested in something else? For example, the Mexican guards in the book were not concerned about alcohol, but they were extremely concerned about firearms.

15. The scene in which the bar in Acuña is infiltrated by the military—do you think this is based on a real event? What would you do in this situation?

16. The book was set in 2010 and depicts a lot of violence happening across the border. What is your impression of the Texas–Mexico border today? Have Hunter's premonitions of the border changing come to fruition or have things settled down? What are your impressions of the cities on the Texas side of the border and how they are affected?

17. How would you describe Hunter's relationship with his friends? Do you have a group of friends like this?

18. How would you describe Hunter's feelings about romantic relationships? Is this a realistic depiction, like your own or that of someone you know? Do you think men and women would see Hunter's attitude differently?

19. Why do you think Hunter approaches those two types of relationships in the ways he does?

20. What do you think Hunter will do about Stacy? Will he pursue a relationship or let it go?

AUTHOR Q & A

Q: What was the inspiration for The West Texas Pilgrimage?

A: The context of the book was inspired by my very own West Texas pilgrimage, an annual trip to West Texas with a special group of guys, "The Flying Burros."

Q: When did you first know you wanted to write a novel?

A: I started my first novel when I was in fifth grade. I had been reading my dad's Tom Clancy novels and wrote a war story. It was a little too graphic for my fifth grade teacher's tastes. I hadn't seriously considered writing a book again until two or three years ago, when I found some inspiration and felt like I had some good stories to tell.

Q: Was it something you had been thinking about for some time, or was it a sudden decision?

A: I have tossed around several ideas for books, and this one was the first to come together.

Q: The descriptions of the locations along the way are vivid and your knowledge of the area and its history seemingly extensive. Have you spent time in West Texas?

A: I fell in love with West Texas while living in Del Rio for three years. I hunted on a ranch outside of Dryden and made several trips to Marathon and Big Bend. I return to West Texas annually with the "Burros" to visit the ash burial site of a great man that loved that country as much as we do.

Q: Are any of the characters in The West Texas Pilgrimage *based on your real-life friends or experiences?*

A: Although the story is completely fictional, my goal was to create an accurate picture of this Texan generation and demographic. I tried to include generationally relevant issues—to include cancer, the War on Terror, border violence, depression, and so on.

Q: Hunter's depression is very realistic. Is this something you've had to deal with in your life or have helped someone else through?

A: I've had my own personal struggles with depression and have known many others that deal with some form of a mental health condition. One objective of the book is to help bring awareness to the fact that everyone reading will know someone impacted by depression or mental illness.

Q: Have you found any working solutions—medication, therapy, a strong support network?

A: All of the above, to include faith in God. Unfortunately, there isn't a silver bullet, but a combination of all of those things has made a tremendous difference in my life. Understanding what "it" is, knowing that there are treatment options, and having faith that things can be better have been key.

Q: The description of OCD is similarly credible. Do you or does someone you know suffer from this as well?

A: I have struggled with OCD since I was in middle school. I wanted to create a character that the millions of people that suffer from OCD could relate to. It is a poorly understood and underdiagnosed anxiety disorder.

Q: Your treatment of grief is also moving and realistic. Is it based on your own loss of a friend and a similar quest?

A: We will all experience the grief of losing someone close at one point or another. It seems that nearly every one of my generation has lost someone to some form of cancer, and the book is dedicated to a great man that was taken too early by cancer.

Q: Have you spent a lot of time in Mexico? The incident in Acuña seems very similar to some real-life events that took place there in 2010. Were you caught up in that event, or was this particular incident somehow important for you to write about?

A: I've lived on or near the border for most of my adult life. There is something about the Texas border with Mexico that I find very intriguing. It has a cultural blend that is unique in its own right. The intrigue may just be that it is still wild in more ways than one. The border has a major influence on anyone growing up in South Texas.

Q: The music in the book is a perfect fit for the story and setting. Is this an extension of your own musical tastes, or was it researched specifically for the book?

A: This is definitely an extension of my own musical tastes, but the songs were carefully selected to fit the various settings. I often tie experiences and memories to songs. It is tough to fully experience a generational culture without musical reference. Interestingly enough, a lot of the music referenced in the book is from previous generations—in relation to the characters' ages—of Texas songwriters. Willie Nelson, Guy Clark, Townes Van Zandt, Steve Earle, and Robert Earl Keen have all had a major influence on my generation and continue to influence the next generation of Texans.

Q: Do you have another book in the works? Anything you can reveal yet?

A: I do have another book in the works, this one based entirely in South Texas. I had done a lot of research for the development of a documentary prior to starting *The West Texas Pilgrimage*, but I have come to the conclusion that the documentary will be more entertaining as a fictional novel. Without going into too much detail, the context will be the story of a corrupt empire created through the guise of a not-for-profit hospital system in South Texas.

ABOUT THE AUTHOR

Matthew Martin Wolthoff lives in McAllen, Texas, with his wife, Lucy Ann, and three children, Hunter Ann, McCoy Martin, and Kerr Dunkin. He grew up in a military family, living all over the world until finding home in South Texas, where he went to high school in San Antonio. He is a graduate of the US Air Force Academy and has a master's degree in business administration from the University of Texas at San Antonio. His parents instilled a passion for reading and writing in him early in life that grows stronger every day. An avid outdoorsman, he finds his inspiration—and peace of mind—in the shallow waters of the Lower Laguna Madre and the wilderness of the South Texas brush country. His first West Texas pilgrimage was in 2010. It was a life-changing event.